PRAISE FOR *THE CONTEST*

"Fans of Preston & Child's Pendergast series will find much to love in *The Contest* from David Golemon. Taut pacing and compelling, interwoven backstories combine in this western with a twist to keep you up all...freaking...night!"
—RICK CHESLER, author of the Tara Shores Thriller series

"Golemon has done it again! *The Contest*'s blend of history and thrills will keep fans of the Event Group series and new readers alike turning the page deep into the night!"
—THUNDER LEVIN, screenwriter of the *Sharknado* TV movies

"As a longtime fan of Golemon, I was hooked from the first page: *The Contest* delivers relentless tension, a cast of morally grey characters, and an atmosphere so unsettling it pulls you in like a haunting legend straight out of America's dark frontier past. If you're looking for a supernatural thriller that keeps your pulse pounding and your mind on a quest for answers, the hunt is over: this is the one from the master of the genre."
—JEFFREY KAFER, original narrator of *The Supernaturals* and co-owner of High Gravity Productions

"Tooth and claw above the rest! *The Contest* is a perfect blend of folklore, horror, and adventure. It should be quintessential reading for all David Golemon fans! For those unfamiliar, this book is a testimony to Golemon's mastery of the art of storytelling!"
—J. KENT HOLLOWAY, international bestselling author of *Death Warmed Over*

ALSO BY DAVID GOLEMON

THE EVENT GROUP THRILLERS
Event
Legend
Ancients
Leviathan
Primeval
Legacy
Ripper
Carpathian
Overlord
The Mountain
The Traveler
Beyond the Sea
Empire of the Dragon
Season of the Witch

THE SUPERNATURALS
The Supernaturals
In the Still of the Night

A NOVEL OF HORROR
FROM THE AMERICAN FRONTIER

THE CONTEST

DAVID GOLEMON

KEYLIGHT BOOKS
AN IMPRINT OF TURNER PUBLISHING COMPANY
Nashville, Tennessee
www.turnerpublishing.com

The Contest
Copyright © 2025 by David Golemon. All rights reserved.

This book or any part thereof may not be reproduced or transmitted in any form or by any means, electronic or mechanical, including photocopying, recording, or by any information storage and retrieval system, without permission in writing from the publisher.

This is a work of fiction. All the characters and events portrayed in this book are either products of the author's imagination or are used fictitiously.

Cover design by David Reuss
Book design by William Ruoto

Library of Congress Cataloging-in-Publication Data
Names: Golemon, David Lynn, author.
Title: The contest: a novel of horror from the American frontier / David L. Golemon.
Description: Nashville, Tennessee : Turner Publishing Company, 2025.
Identifiers: LCCN 2024038171 (print) | LCCN 2024038172 (ebook) | ISBN 9798887980522 (paperback) | ISBN 9798887980539 (hardcover) | ISBN 9798887980546 (epub)
Subjects: LCGFT: Horror fiction. | Novels.
Classification: LCC PS3607.O48598 C66 2025 (print) | LCC PS3607.O48598 (ebook) | DDC 813/.6—dc23/eng/20240816
LC record available at https://lccn.loc.gov/2024038171
LC ebook record available at https://lccn.loc.gov/2024038172

Printed in the United States of America

For my granddaughters, Kiera and Everly

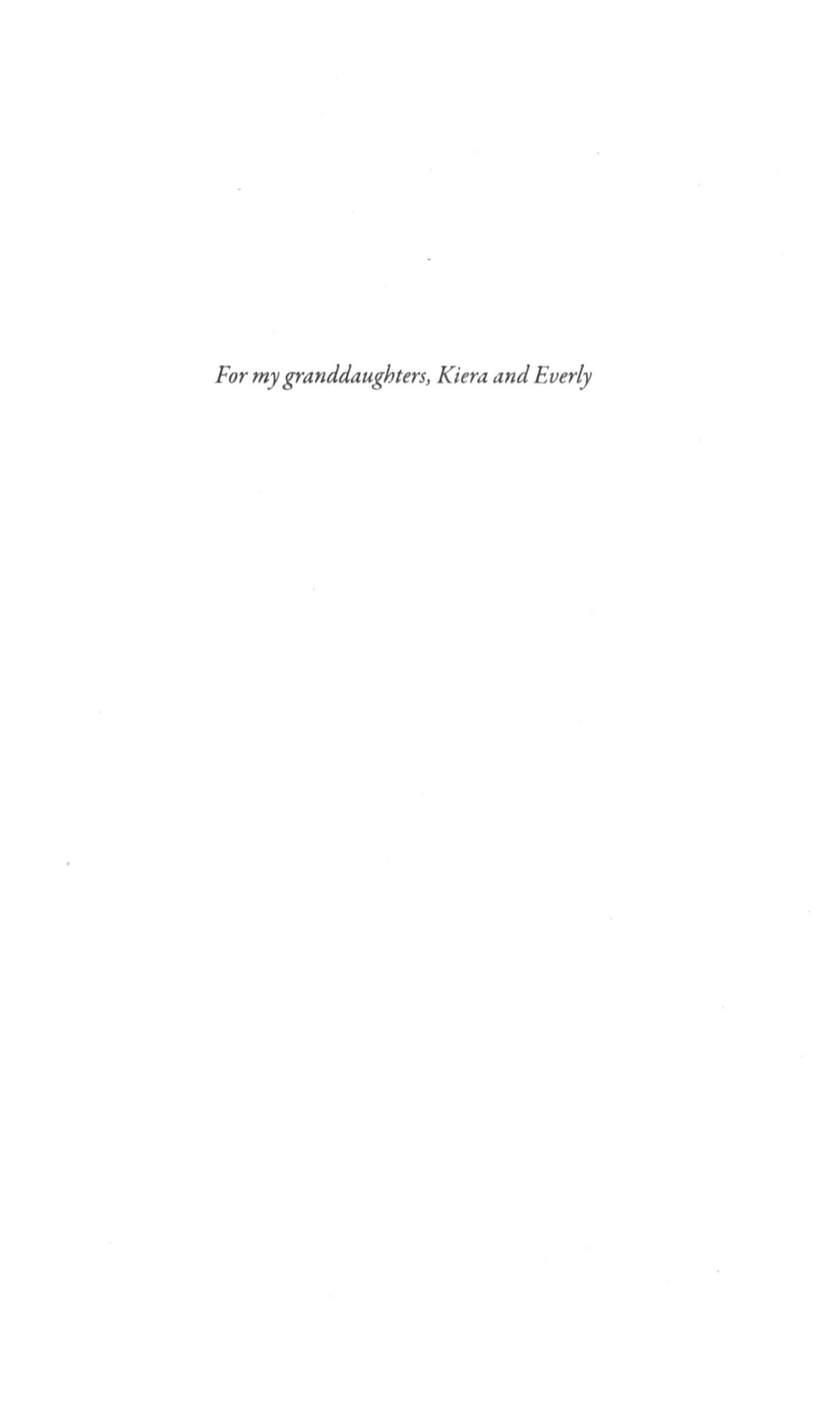

PROLOGUE

MONTANA TERRITORY

The first snow of the year caught the small encampment by surprise after an unseasonably warm fall. Powder quickly covered the five lodges until the later hours, when the skies opened in earnest. Not having been this far north of the Yellowstone so late during the hunting season in several years, the men had underestimated the omens the Lakota, Ogallala, and Hunkpapa medicine men had warned about a month before.

They sat around the warm fire and ate a simple meal of venison and small cakes of US Army–supplied sorghum and cornmeal. The talk between them was quiet, mindful of the camp's women, who sat to the far side of the large lodge and silently fed their children. The men kept their discussions to a minimum: the winter encampment near Fort Laramie, the delayed traveling in favor of an extra month of hunting to supplement their winter supplies, and the summer gathering with extended family and friends they had left behind.

The group had spent most of the hot months at the area known to the Lakota Sioux as Greasy Grass, harvesting as many buffalo, deer, and elk as they could at the confluence of the Little Big Horn River and Gooseberry Creek. The eight adult warriors only hoped they hadn't waited too long to take their families south for the winter. Maybe their share of Indian agency beef, supplied by the US government through the auspices of the Fort Laramie Treaty signed in 1851, would last the journey.

Although leaderless through the view of white culture, not one Sioux warrior ever told another what to do in life. However, there was one man who held the most sway—the voice responsible for not following the tribal advice of the camp elders and not participating in the buffalo hunt of late summer with the rest of their people. The greatest of Lakota warriors, Running Horse. A proud man who had always been against the Fort Laramie Treaty and the accepting of the white man's charity, he thought Chief Red Cloud and many other elders were fools for signing it.

It had been his decision to stay with his family and a few other warriors, to hunt through the fall season and refuse to beg for sustenance from the people responsible for stealing their ancestral lands. But now he felt as though he had misled his small following into choices that would leave their larders empty for the winter.

"In the morning, we shall break camp, if all agree." Running Horse looked at the other men around him for their consensus. Heavier snow penetrated the lodge's fire flap at its top. His look told the others of his despondency over his earlier bad decision. He tossed the remains of the corn cake into the fire.

"There is no shame in this, Running Horse. Every tribe that signed or did not sign the white man's paper is bending to the hard will of Father Winter. There can be no cause greater than feeding our people."

"Broken Gun speaks truth," said Kicking Badger, the elder of the small band.

"This land south of the Greasy Grass has never been hunted out before." Running Horse swatted the rear of his young son,

THE CONTEST

encouraging him to join his mother for food. "I failed to see sign. I have failed to understand. Even Brother Wolf is starving."

"Perhaps it was the Crow? They invade every sacred place of the Lakota and take the animals of the forest," the elder said, looking into the fire.

"I would agree, if the Crow could hunt," Running Horse said facetiously.

The rest of the men chuckled and nodded.

The old man smiled. "This is true."

"The tracks and other sign are what confuse me." Running Horse grew serious. "Tracks the likes of which I have never seen before."

"The greatest hunter and tracker is confused? Doom has surely arrived for our people."

The others found humor in the old man's calming jest.

Running Horse respected Kicking Badger and took no offense to his gentle ribbing.

"Yes, yes, some great hunter and tracker. I cannot even find sign of elk. The small creatures like deer and rabbit have left this fertile place. Kicking Badger, you have been a hunter here for many, many seasons. Have you ever beheld a barren fall such as this?"

"Running Horse is a kind soul. He accuses me of being old and makes it sound as if it is praise."

The men laughed again.

Kicking Badger grew serious. "In answer to your question, my son, no. This is unusual for such a fertile and lesser-known valley, I agree. The animals of the forest have vanished. As you say, our brother the wolf have left."

The men agreed, except for one. This man sat slightly aloof from the others and stared into the warm fire.

"Then it is decided. We go to Fort Laramie and act as beggars through the winter moons." The youngest warrior of the group, Fallen Tree, stood and left the lodge.

The others watched the irritated boy.

"He means nothing by his anger, Running Horse. Fallen Tree has never had to watch his wife and children go through a hungry winter as we have. He still argues for a raid on the Crow or Arikara."

"Make war because we cannot hunt for a living? The young fool knows neither of starvation nor war." Running Horse shook his head.

The men around the fire quieted, and the wind howled. Father Winter's breath made haunting music through the still-full pine trees of the valley. The men listened. Running Horse cocked his head at the soft, flute-like notes before the cold snatched the sound away.

"Winter is starting to sing a sad song," he said.

Kicking Badger began to agree but stopped when the four dogs traveling with them erupted into an angry wail of warning.

"Crow, Arikara?" Kicking Badger asked as all the men stood. "Perhaps it is they who make music in the night?"

"Too early in the night for a raid," Running Horse said.

His wife was the first to react of the women feeding their children. She hurriedly tossed Running Horse a seven-shot Spencer carbine. The weapon had been "gifted" to him by a foolish American soldier scout who had mistakenly feared Running Horse was stalking him. One night after camping, the frightened man abandoned his horse, saddle, and weaponry in his flight to escape the clutches of the "savage Indian" doing nothing more than observing the man from afar. The other warriors had retrieved several older breech-loading weapons and bows.

The men left the warmth of the lodge as the camp's dogs continued barking their warnings.

The wind had picked up, and the thick snow was falling, covering the camp with a whiteness Indians of every nation feared. Even the strange reverberation streamed through the trees again. An exotic sound no one had ever heard before joined the flute or whistle. It was sweet and accompanied the other with an almost hypnotic harmony.

Then the melody, as before, vanished on the night's wind.

Running Horse, with a quick wave of his hand, silenced the dogs and then stopped and listened. He went to a knee, examining an area near the largest of the lodges. Small footprints were clearly outlined in the fresh snow, as if unheard and unseen forces had scouted the warrior's small camp while they ate their scant meal. Running Horse tracked the human prints to the tree line, quickly counting over fifty differing sets. He cocked the Spencer rifle.

The young warrior, Fallen Tree, exited his lodge with his ancient muzzle-loading rifle. He had just rammed a ball home and was placing the ramrod into its holder. The other seven men paused, ears straining. Fallen Tree shook his head in embarrassment at his overly cautious friends but eventually joined them and stood watchful in front of his small lodge. The wind freshened, and even heavier snow began to fall.

Cotton ball–sized snowflakes floated from the night sky and swirled to a blinding fury. The world became silent, and even the cold wind stopped so suddenly, the men were positive the world had somehow changed since the sun had fallen earlier in the day. The dogs whined like something in the surrounding woods frightened them.

Running Horse silenced them once more and waved the dogs ahead to seek out whatever they had sensed in the night. His eyes moved easily from camp to tree line, and Running Horse had the distinct impression they were being watched by many eyes. With his Spencer cocked and ready, he eased away from the large lodge. Several others notched arrows, and the rest brought their rifles up.

Even the heavy snow stopped.

"I have never heard it this quiet. It's as if the Great Spirit has left this place." Kicking Badger scanned the clearing.

Before anyone realized what was happening, Fallen Tree was attacked. By the time the men of the camp turned toward the loud grunt, he had vanished, his muzzleloader left lying in the snow. His small lodge shook, and Fallen Tree screamed in pain and horror from inside. A large rip appeared in the skin, and Fallen Tree was thrown from its interior. He hit the snow and skid to a stop in front of the other men.

His head was gone from the nose up. Blood spurted and spread onto the pristine snow.

Running Horse aimed his carbine at the lodge and fired blindly. Three bullet holes appeared in the buffalo skin.

Silence.

He lowered his weapon.

An animalistic roar erupted, shaking the silent world around them. Snow hanging from the branches of trees fell, and pine needles cascaded to the white earth. The other lodges shook. The hobbled horses reared and screamed in terror. They lost their ropes and sprinted into the night with wide, animal-panicked eyes.

"Bear!" Kicking Badger screamed. He pulled his stone-topped club from his belt and went charging at the shaking lodge of Fallen Tree.

Running Horse watched helplessly. In all his years of the hunt, he had never seen a bear act like this. He hurriedly ran after Kicking Badger just as the small lodge exploded with a power no bear could generate. The pine poles shot into the air; the buffalo hide flying skyward.

The sight froze the six warriors' blood.

Standing where the lodge had been was a creature no legend of the Lakota could ever match. The beast bellowed. Still, Kicking Badger charged.

"No!" Running Horse screamed. He turned and rushed toward his wife standing by the lodge flap. He aggressively gestured for her to take the children and other women and run for the cover of the trees.

The animal towered well over eight feet in height and was on two legs, seemingly prepared for the wild charge of the old warrior. With raised battle club, Kicking Badger attacked, even as three high-velocity balls slammed into the thick, black hide of the creature. With no ill effect from the bullets, the beast reached out with a six-inch-clawed hand and swiped at Kicking Badger. The warrior flew into the closest tree, where the horses had been hobbled, and his old body came apart.

Arrow after arrow and bullet after bullet tore into the creature, who was seemingly unharmed by each assault to its body. It shook its massive head, and saliva flew. With self-illuminated eyes blazing yellow and ringed in red, it continued the assault on the small camp in earnest.

Running Horse fired the Spencer until he ejected his last casing. He turned the rifle over and charged the creature, intending to strike out. The beast tore into the men with savage fury, caring not for any form of mercy. This was no mere wild animal fighting and defending territory for fear of man. This was a hell-sent monster that enjoyed rending men to shreds.

When the beast went low to attack a charging warrior, three arrows whistled through the air and buried deep in its chest. This still didn't slow the animal. The great muzzle of the giant crushed the skull of one warrior, and the claws nearly sliced another man in two.

The creature was off-balance with its last blow. Running Horse slammed the butt of the Spencer into its head. The skull broke with the crunch of bone, but that only seemed to fill the beast with rage. It swung back and caught Running Horse in the sternum, sending him hurtling.

With no air in his lungs, Running Horse slammed into the snow-covered ground and rolled. He tried to draw life-sustaining breaths back into his bruised body. The creature roared and continued its bloody work. Running Horse shook his head to clear it. He rose to his knees, pulled his knife, and blindly rushed the monster sent from below.

The animal dispatched the last warrior and watched Running Horse bravely lunge forward. Running Horse, limping with a broken leg, screamed the warrior's battle cry with knife held high. The creature seemed to be smiling, tilting its head in wonder at the audacity of the warrior, perhaps admiring the misguided heroics of the Sioux.

The knife came down and into the beast, just above the heart. The animal let out a yelp like a hurt canine. The creature slapped Running Horse to the ground, ready to pounce, when the four dogs who had initially run in fear hit the monster. To the injured Running Horse, the fight between dogs and beast looked like ants battling a wild boar. The dogs were tossed off and killed one at a time.

The wintery night gave way to a thunderous storm. Sleet replaced snow, and lightning streaked the Montana skies.

Running Horse's mind drifted, and the heavy sleet pelted his bloody face while he lay on the earth. The only sound was the crunch of snow.

The massive feet of the beast came into the line of his limited vision. They were heavily padded and clawed, shaped like those of a dog. Running Horse felt as if he were dreaming. The giant's taloned hand wrapped tightly around his neck, and his body was raised into the air.

Running Horse, the greatest warrior of the Lakota, prepared himself for death.

The beast lifted until the warrior was looking into the hate-filled eyes of a nightmare. The creature shook him, and Running Horse's eyes started to dim and tunnel.

The screams and cries of the women came from somewhere in the woods, in flight from the massacre. Running Horse fought to turn his head. The warrior wanted to see his wife and only son, but the monster wouldn't allow it. The creature shook Running Horse once more as if to get his attention.

The blazing yellow eyes went from the face of the smashed and bloody warrior to the frightened women and children. The great head of the animal turned, and with its free hand, it gestured to something or someone Running Horse couldn't see.

The laughter of children and footsteps echoed through the night. The beast had sent something after the camp's women and children.

The hate-filled eyes, dripping with rainwater, returned their focus to Running Horse. The monster pulled out the knife protruding from its chest. The spawn of hell dropped it, and its horrid grin grew. He turned Running Horse to face the sounds of the fleeing women and children.

Close to fifty small, human-like creatures pursued Running

Horse's family, backlit by a bolt of lightning. The nightmarish horde spread out into the woods. The beast quickly pulled Running Horse away and opened its long muzzle, exposing teeth no man on the North American continent had ever witnessed. It growled deeply and tossed the great hunter and tracker aside as if he were nothing more than a leaf fallen from a tree. The giant feet stepped over Running Horse, and the creature vanished into the sleet-soaked night, following the same path as the minions it had sent to find the women and children.

Running Horse was losing the last flicker of consciousness. With the deep laceration on his face pulsing blood, the only function of a mind in shock was him bearing witness to the sounds of his family being torn to pieces, their screams echoing through the cold. Just when his eyes started to close, he beheld the last strange sight of this long night.

Sitting in the pine trees like a murder of crows were a few of the small, black-clad forms of the human-like minions—diminutive, hooded men watching the slaughter with grinning mouths, wide and hungry. They left the trees and ran after the beast, with the exception of two small, white-faced creatures.

Running Horse's consciousness continued to fade. The remaining creatures looked upon him sadly and hopped from the tree. The slightly larger of the two dropped something from its dark sleeve. As the man-like creature retrieved it, it looked like a wooden flute. The instrument was not unlike the one Running Horse had made his oldest son the summer before.

His world faded to black and was gone.

PART ONE

THE CONTESTANTS

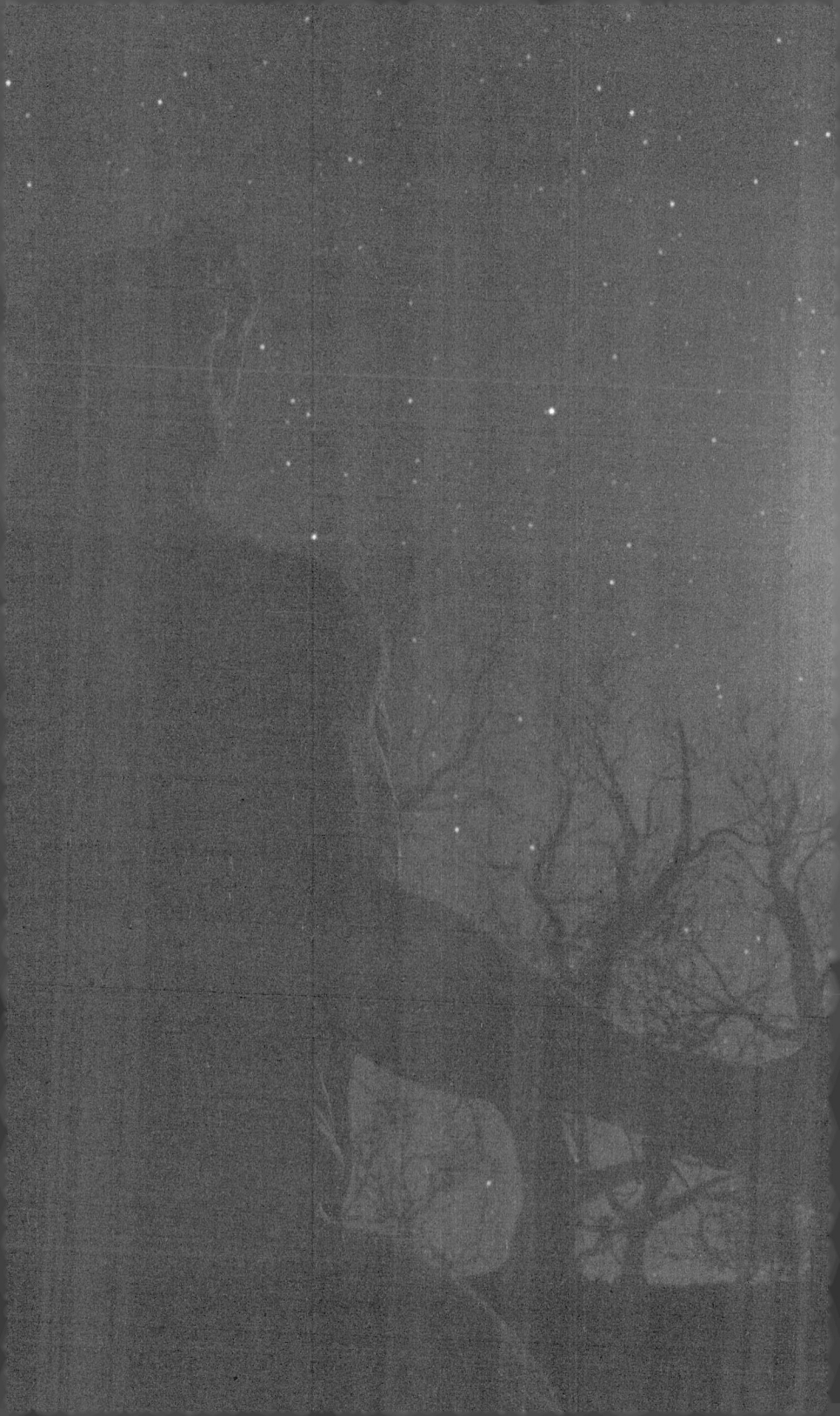

CHAPTER ONE

PARIS, FRANCE 1865

The meeting would take place in the once-proud law offices of Phillipe Darnaux, of Darnaux, Krell, and d'Aboville. The principal head of the firm was in his final days before retirement. The case he was handling was his last and would raise his small firm out of the red for the first time in three years. Darnaux, Krell, and d'Aboville would be turned over to his partners since Darnaux had no next of kin to take the reins. He drew up his retirement requirements for his partners to countersign the moment the meeting with his client ended. With pen in hand, he had but to place his signature, and his law career would be at an end.

Darnaux laid the pen down, savoring the moment before signing. He would depart with honor, knowing he had saved his law firm and thus his reputation. After decades of hiring out to swindlers and deviants—also his own malfeasance—he would retire clean.

A knock sounded on his door.

"Come," the portly Darnaux called out.

"Sir, your twelve-thirty appointment has arrived."

Darnaux took a deep breath, nodded, and stood to greet the representative of his client.

His secretary opened the door and exchanged words with someone in the outer office before allowing the gentleman in.

Darnaux extended his hand to the small man in the top hat and gloves, admiring the way he dressed. For a man of servile employment, the gentleman must have been exceptionally well compensated.

"Monsieur Alexandros."

For the tenth time since first meeting him, Alexandros did not shake Darnaux's hand. Instead of the greeting, Alexandros removed his hat and placed a small satchel on the carpet. Only then did he ease into the chair in front of Darnaux's desk. Alexandros set the hat on his knee, which he crossed over his right leg.

Darnaux was nonplussed. He had ceased trying to figure out the manservant since making his acquaintance over three years before.

"I am happy, Monsieur, you received my cable. I must say, you made excellent time arriving from out east. I hope your journey was a comfortable one?"

"As pleasant as a private railcar can be." Alexandros took off his white gloves and tucked them in the top hat. "Since I received your telegram, I must assume your firm has completed the task as contracted for?"

"Indeed, we have. I must say, it was one of the more difficult assignments this firm has taken on in many—"

"May I see the list, please?"

Darnaux was again unbothered by the interruption. In the past, before his streak of bad luck, he had been cut off by the very best French royalty and society had to offer, so why should the representative of a Rumanian lord be any different? Darnaux opened an accordion-like folder and handed his visitor the requested document.

"All seven have been located?"

"Yes, at great expense and exhausting travel. My overseas associates had great difficulty, what with the war ending in America and men scattered to the wind. I'm sure you understand our hardship?"

Alexandros looked up from the list. "That does not concern me nor my employer, Monsieur Darnaux. Or them, as a matter of fact." He nodded at the window and the dreary and misty day outside the glass.

"Good god, do those things travel with you?"

Five small, white faces stared in at the meeting, their eyes darkened and veins clearly seen through their paper-thin, pale skin. The bald heads were mercifully covered in the black robes they always wore. One even smiled at the Frenchman. They sat on the windowsill in a crouch, like predators awaiting their prey.

The lawyer got up from his chair and closed the blinds, shutting out the ghastly sight.

"They, too, will soon be off to America to assist their master and brethren. My employer breeds them, you see, and they are all very dear to him."

Darnaux returned to his chair in disgust at the diminutive human-like beings providing security for the manservant and, evidently, the Rumanian lord himself—a vision burning a reservation into the future nightmares of the attorney. Breeding small dwarves was not something they would ever conceive of in the West, he thought with disdain.

The first time he had met the man from Rumania, the task had been simple and the advance payment for their services exceptionally high. The firm was to gather a list of certain men and was contracted to get full backgrounds on their seven histories and current whereabouts. Some of the names given were recognizable, even a few quite famous. Each, as noted in their histories, highly valued their privacy, either due to their fame or their legal status.

The man placed the list on Darnaux's desk and reached for the satchel he had brought in with him. Alexandros pulled out seven refined envelopes sealed with wax and doubly secured by a satin ribbon. Each name was scripted in the most delicate and fluid hand, and the envelopes were three times the size of a normal letter. He placed the shiny red envelopes on the desk next to the list.

"This, of course, will be the last function your firm completes for my employer. After today's meeting, you will destroy all reference to our initial contract and the negotiation of same."

"As per our last discussion."

The man looked annoyed by Darnaux confirming his just-uttered words. Instead of a rebuke, he again reached into the satchel and retrieved a smaller envelope. This was the one Phillipe Darnaux had been waiting on. Alexandros handed it to him.

"This is your payment and a copy of the bank draft for the contest winnings. The one million dollars in contestant winnings is to be paid out in American gold double eagles to avoid any monetary forgeries."

The look at Darnaux was far beyond insulting. His past discretions were brought to the fore in unvoiced accusation. If it had been anyone else, Darnaux would have had the man shot. Or so he bravely bragged in his innermost thoughts.

"The gold has already been deposited by my employer in the Bank of Boston, of which said firm will be awarding the prize upon completion of the contest. Your payment of one million francs is drawn on my employer's account with Banque Courtois in Toulouse upon the successful completion and confirmation of delivery to the contestants the engraved invitations, as named on the list. Now, as I do not see the contestants in Europe and Asia as a problem, my employer is concerned about the travel habits of the American invitees. Are your contacts in America adequate for the challenge of finding and delivering the invitations?"

"I assure you, sir, the company contracted is based out of Chicago, and the owner of the agency guarantees one hundred percent delivery. Alan Pinkerton is a fine man, and his detective agency is very professional in manner and confidentiality."

The Rumanian placed his gloves on his hands. "That will be your contact's concern, as my employer will be handling all matters from this point forward on a more"—he smiled—"personal basis. I shall be taking the *India Star* liner to America to oversee the contest." Alexandros stood up and retrieved his cane and valise. "And Monsieur Darnaux, I am no fool. I believe it was Mr. Pinkerton who was responsible for securing the life of President Lincoln. Let's hope he has better success with the delivery of a few invitations, shall we?"

He again faced the door but then stopped.

"Now, one last, very important thing. I have not heard your report on my master's brother." Alexandros pivoted, and there was not one ounce of humor on his darkened features. "Have you located him?"

"Mr. Pinkerton reported they lost him west of St. Louis. He suspects him to have hidden himself in the wilds of Indian Territory."

"Yes, it is as we assumed. We suspect his location." This time, the servant *did* smile. "You see, sir, we also have our contacts in a very small world. On behalf of my lord, good day to you." He started to leave.

"Where is your master?" Darnaux asked, rising from his chair.

The Rumanian stopped, and his shoulders slumped.

"If I may inquire…"

"He's been in America for quite some time. He's rather excited to get the contest started—hopefully within the next two years. He has a few arrangements to make that impact on the contest. An invite that is not on the list needs to be persuaded to accept the challenge, as the monetary reward for winning the contest holds no interest for this individual. I understand the gentleman has already been contacted and may now find interest in the contest. Good day, Monsieur Darnaux. I expect to never meet again." Alexandros began to open the door but paused and, without turning, said, "If something fails to happen, it won't be me you see. It will be either my employer or our tiny friends outside the window. We wouldn't want that now, would we?"

Darnaux glanced to the window and the small creatures he knew were there. He directed his attention back to Alexandros, watched the man leave, and shook his head in wonder. Darnaux reached for his payment and placed it in his coat pocket. Out of curiosity, he lifted the first of the invitations and inspected it.

The metal-looking style of construction was like no envelope he had ever seen. The handwriting on the front was beautiful in detail and easy to read. Darnaux set the invitation, with the wax seal and the coat of arms he didn't recognize, back down. Whatever stamp had been used to mark the seal must have been old because he couldn't tell if the symbol was of a dog or a wolf.

Another knock sounded on the door, and his secretary stepped in. "Monsieur, if you'll not be needing me, I'll just step out for a bit of lunch before the rain starts in earnest."

Darnaux gathered the gilded envelopes and handed them to his young assistant. "Yes, before lunch, deliver these letters to the

Clemenceau Detective Agency and inform them to commence with the deliveries. Then make sure the second batch is delivered to the post office for immediate delivery to Chicago, Illinois, America. Then you may take the rest of the day. I won't be needing you."

"Yes, Monsieur," the boy said. He took the seven invitations and left the office.

Darnaux returned to the window and slowly raised the blinds. The small creatures had vanished silently, like they always did. The Frenchman looked over Paris. It had just started to rain hard, and while he watched the River Seine, he wondered just what sort of contest could involve the unheard-of amount of one million American dollars in winnings.

LONDON, ENGLAND

The First and Second Invitees

Chief Inspector Robert Tensilwith watched the flat from a fog-choked alley. Unable to discern much other than the inconsistent, flickering gaslight, he worried he had missed his suspect. He removed his pocket watch and noted the time—12:02 a.m., which meant if the man kept to his schedule, he would be exiting the flat at any moment. After two long years, Tensilwith had cornered the man he had suspected from the very beginning.

The chief inspector snapped his watch closed and gestured to the two policemen standing security.

"Gentlemen, it's time. Signal your fellows to make the arrest."

"Sir!"

Tensilwith watched the young officers move out of the alley, where they were met by four more of London's finest armed with brand-new Martini-Henry rifles. They ran through the fog and up the steps of the run-down flat. The chief inspector took his time while he followed. He wanted Sir Niles Van-Pattenson to see his face last and know it was he who had figured out his murderous game. Tensilwith slowly climbed the outside steps.

One of his men exited the building and vomited over the stone banister. Concerned, Tensilwith eased by the suddenly ill officer. He was shocked when the young man grabbed his coat and stopped him from progressing up the steps.

"Don't go in there, Chief Inspector." The boy wiped his mouth on his uniform sleeve. "It will do you no good to see that."

"See what? Did the bastard hang himself? Take the coward's way out?"

"Sir, he's not in the flat. It's a—"

The young policeman leaned over the railing and vomited again.

The next man up the steps was also wiping his mouth after doing the same thing. Only this man was the vastly more experienced Sergeant Collingwood, a man the chief inspector had known for ten years. Collingwood took Tensilwith by the shoulders and looked him in the eyes.

"Don't go up there, Robert. Please, let me handle this."

"Have all my officers gone mad? Let me by!"

The large sergeant refused to allow the chief inspector to pass. "If I must place you on your backside, sir, I will. You are not going up there."

"*My* suspect, *my* arrest!"

"Robert, Sir Niles is not there. He left you a calling card."

The chief inspector experienced true fear for the first time in his professional career. "What are you talking about, Sergeant?"

"Sir, it's your wife."

The blood drained from the chief inspector's face. He turned and struggled to get free of the hold on him, but other men came from the flat and assisted. Finally, the four of them wrestled the chief inspector to the cold, wet steps.

It was forty minutes later, and the street was alive with police activity and curious neighbors. Uniformed and plain-clothed men came and went, and a man sat in the open carriage of Police Commissioner Lord Gerald Highsmith. While the officers removed the shroud-covered body from the poorly maintained flat, the chief inspector tried to leave the coach but was again restrained by the commissioner's men. Tensilwith let out a wail that would have frozen the hearts of the most seasoned soldier in Her Majesty's service.

An angry commissioner stopped the men carrying the body and furiously scolded them. A bloodied and mutilated arm had slid from beneath the blue shroud. The commissioner removed his hat and wiped beads of nervous sweat from his brow. Highsmith took a kerchief and cleaned the blood from his hand after re-covering the arm. He turned, placed the hat back on, and walked to the carriage.

"I'm sorry you had to see that, Chief Inspector. Bad show that was."

"Maybe...maybe it's not Elizabeth," Tensilwith said, almost as a plea.

The commissioner couldn't bring himself to face Tensilwith. He coughed to clear his throat. "Robert, I'm afraid it was. The coroner's assistant said she has been dead for several hours, at the very least. While you were briefing your men at the Yard on the procedures of arrest, Elizabeth was taken from your home and brought here. She's been in the flat since you arrived. Sir Niles has been gone for several hours after his despicable deed was completed." The commissioner stopped the sergeant who was coming to check on his friend. "I have given orders for the arrest of Sir Niles Van-Pattenson. He now knows he can't hide from this bloody mess, so I suspect he'll try flight instead of national and familial embarrassment." Highsmith directed his attention to the angry sergeant. "I want men at every train station and commercial shipping dock."

The sergeant, with a last look at the chief inspector, took the police commissioner by the arm and pulled him away from his friend.

"Sir Niles is obviously insane, sir. He will not come peacefully."

The commissioner glanced at the grieving chief inspector, then back at the gruff sergeant.

"No, I suspect not. We need not bring in doctors and mental specialists so Sir Niles can get off on medical technicality. Besides, it will save the queen some rather awkward questioning. So, Sergeant, make sure justice is delivered before all of that legal mumbo jumbo, shall we? Do you get my meaning?"

The sergeant opened his coat and allowed the commissioner to see the Webley pistol in its holster.

"Then I believe we have an understanding, Sergeant."

It was five days later that Chief Inspector Robert Tensilwith watched his beloved wife of three years lying on a shrouded platform, waiting to be placed into the wet, cold earth. The mourners were from all police precincts in the city, and even the Queen Victoria's representative, Princess Alice, bore witness to the gathering.

After the many condolences, Tensilwith was approached by his oldest friend, Sergeant Haskell Collingwood, the man who had sworn to the commissioner he would find and kill the murderous Sir Niles Van-Pattenson. The chief inspector accepted the offered handshake after a disquieting moment of accusing eyes. The sergeant had yet to locate Sir Niles. Tensilwith walked away from the flower-draped casket of his wife.

"Chief Inspector, it is I who bear the responsibility of allowing Sir Niles to escape England."

"He would not have done so if I hadn't been removed from the case by pompous asses who know nothing of tracking men down."

"Sir, the commissioner thought it best that—"

"Do you have something to say, Sergeant?"

"The commissioner has ordered the release of the rented flat back to the landlord, sir. When making my last inspection of the apartment before turning over the crime scene, I came across this partially hidden in the tattered rug that your"—he looked down at his feet—"your wife was rolled up in."

"What is it?" Tensilwith asked when he saw the blood-stained article.

"A receipt of service." The sergeant handed him a small piece of paper. "It was for the service of Jones and McCartney Detective Agency right here in London. They have a rather dubious history of dealing with lowlifes of the city, they have. I tracked them down and have an interesting bit of news, sir. I figured you would prefer the commissioner not to be involved. I owe you at least that much."

The sergeant turned and waved a man over. His umbrella hid his face, and even while the man approached, he refused to make eye contact with either the sergeant or the chief inspector.

"This is Liam Jones." The sergeant roughly removed the umbrella from the man's hands. "A former policeman who was discharged for working closely with gambling criminals as an enforcer and collector. His partner was charged with even worse crimes in the past. He has decided to cooperate with the Yard on this case. Haven't you?" The sergeant emphasized his claim with a shake of the man's arm.

"Yes, you bloody wanker. I should report this manhandling to—"

"Shut up and show the inspector!"

The man appeared terrified of Sergeant Collingwood. He reached into his coat and brought out a duplicate of the receipt. "I personally delivered a small package to Sir Niles Van-Pattenson six days ago with instructions for absolute discretion."

"And this package was...?" the chief inspector asked.

"I do not know. It was fancied up like nothing I ever seen and something a well-placed gentleman would receive."

"Go on!" the sergeant admonished.

"I was hired to deliver two of these letters to two different men. The second gentleman was deceased, and thus I was unable to make delivery. But I did notice that Sir Niles seemed very happy upon reading *his* message."

"Give the chief inspector the package of the deceased man, you blithering idiot!" The sergeant didn't wait, however, and ripped the man's coat while removing it himself.

"This letter was the exact duplicate of the invitation that Sir Niles received. I was supposed to destroy it if undeliverable, but… but—"

"The unscrupulous bastard thought he saw profit in not doing so," the sergeant said angrily.

"An invitation?" Tensilwith lifted the bright red letter with the already broken wax seal. With a glance at the low-life detective, he opened it and pulled out the handwritten note. He read and reread it, then looked the private detective in the eye. "And this is an exact duplicate of the same letter Sir Niles received?"

"Chief Inspector, I deserve some form of compensation for my trouble."

Collingwood placed the Webley pistol to the side of Jones's head and cocked it. "Perhaps I should explain to you that we no longer consider this a matter for the police. It is more in line with a personal endeavor of which you are generously offering your assistance."

Tensilwith lowered Sergeant Collingwood's arm. "Answer the question, or I will allow my friend to shoot you."

"Yes, you bloody cheap bastards." Jones leaned away from Collingwood. "The two invitations are identical."

The chief inspector nodded at the sergeant. The burly man pushed the private detective away, emphasizing their conversation and business was concluded by tossing his umbrella at him. "The next time I see you, it won't be such a pleasant encounter."

The cowed man left the cemetery, and Collingwood turned to face his old friend. "What now?"

Tensilwith held the bright red envelope and faced his wife's grave. He walked over to the unburied casket draped in flowers, removed his badge from his vest, and lightly placed it on top, closing his eyes in a final goodbye.

"Sir?"

"Thank you, Sergeant, for not telling the commissioner."

Sergeant Collingwood gazed at the badge lying on the bed of flowers and then back at Tensilwith.

"What will you do now?"

"I believe I hold an invitation to meet my quarry, Sir Niles Van-Pattenson. Whoever sent this invitation obviously knew who the murderer Sir Niles was and what he became. I now have interest in two men. Sergeant, one last favor, if you would?" He looked at the addressee on the red invitation.

"Anything, Chief Inspec—Robert."

"I need the background information—and get with some of our low-life friends here in London and get me some forged identification papers—for a Lord Colonel Gerard Langley, late of Her Majesty's armed forces in India. Also known as one of the greatest game hunters...rather famous. And luckily dead. That is why our crooked detective failed to find him. Let us just hope our mysterious host of this so-called contest in the wilds of America has never met the good colonel and wouldn't know him on sight."

"Where are you going, sir?"

"A place called Wyoming in America. Cheyenne, to be precise."

MATO GROSSO DO SUL, BRAZIL

The Third Invitee

The man watched the gauchos herding the two hundred head of

cattle from the river to their grazing pasture on the side of a gently sloping hill. He was patient, lowering his small frame to the long grass. The man lay on his back, picked up the American-printed penny dreadful, and started reading about the exploits of the famous buffalo hunter and Indian killer, "Kit" Carson. While the tales of the American frontier were a basic blend of outright fabrication and unsubstantiated rumor, coupled with a New York writer's fanciful imagination, he highly suspected the adventures he read were nothing more than image building.

Frank "Porteguee" Morales styled himself after the American frontiersmen he read about. With his tasseled black hat and equally black, silver-threaded and stitched clothing, Porteguee Frank adjusted the gun belt holding the twin silver-plated Navy Colts and rested under the large tree.

Over the three years he had been an enforcer for the fledgling cattle industry in Brazil, he had killed over seventy-seven rustlers. Not one of the thieves had been brought in alive—the way the association of cattle barons liked it. The ranchers were their own law, and Porteguee Frank was their judge, jury, and executioner. At the age of twenty-three, he had killed more men than any person in the Americas. Frank never took chances when someone had the ability to shoot back. With his reputation growing, the newspapers in Rio had proclaimed him the "Angel of Death."

It wasn't long before the gauchos headed off for their supper. He carefully placed the red ribbon in the book so as not to lose his place and then yawned. Frank stood, stretched, and walked to his black roan. He placed the book carefully into a saddlebag and hoisted himself into the silver concho–studded saddle. Frank rode to the edge of the hill and watched the gauchos vanish over a far ridge. He calmly waited atop his horse.

It wasn't a long intermission.

Just before the sun started to sink below the far hills, he spied on his rustlers. Frank shook his head, jostling the black furry balls of the tassels lining his hat. He slowly pulled the Navy Colts and checked their cap and ball loads. Frank twirled both weapons—having read that John C. Frémont, the American frontiersman, did—and placed them lightly into the oiled holsters. But according to his years of reading, the story told of Frémont was an outright lie because the frontiersman rarely used a pistol of any kind.

He watched as a woman and two teenage boys eased into the herd of grazing cattle. For many weeks, he had suspected the thieves were not professional rustlers. The cattle never vanished in great numbers. It was reported by the rancher only one or two a month were being taken from his land. That usually meant the thieves were nothing more than starving peasants from the local villages. Frank assumed the woman and her two boys would butcher one of the cows and sell the other. By the looks of them, ragged and starving, they more than likely sold much more of the butchered cow than they kept.

Better yet, none of the three were armed.

He spurred his horse forward at a leisurely gait. With silver conchos shining, Porteguee Frank rode through the last of the day's brightness. Before the first teenage boy was no longer blinded by the setting sun, Frank fired through the boy's forehead with one aimed shot from a great distance. The mother screamed out in surprise while her second boy was down in front of her. The cattle grazing on the slope started running. The poorly dressed mother tried to get to her two boys, when more gunfire rang out. She fell to the ground, a clean bullet hole in her back.

Porteguee Frank again spun the Navy Colt while holstering it and started to dismount. The second boy was trying to crawl to his mother's side. Frank shook his head in irritation at having missed his killing mark. He walked up and used his shiny black boot to kick the boy over onto his back.

"Sua mãe está morta." Frank went to a knee and looked the child over.

The black-haired boy couldn't have been more than twelve years old. He buried his head into the thick grass upon learning his mother was dead.

Frank stood, removed the Colt he hadn't used, and cocked it. The boy looked into the eyes of Porteguee Frank. He didn't cry out, seemed ready for what was coming. Frank stooped once more, removing a kerchief and placing it over the boy's sad eyes. He put the barrel of the Colt against the child's head and fired a shot through his temple. Frank wadded up the red, now-smoking kerchief and tossed it away. He stood and twirled the silver-plated pistol before holstering it.

"Numbers seventy-eight, seventy-nine, and eighty," he said proudly, stretching and yawning.

When reading about the recent carnage in the United States, Frank always wondered what kind of damage he could have done if involved in the great American war of rebellion. But he always corrected his thinking when he realized soldiers in both armies shot back. Very few would lie down at the sight of the smallish man from Brazil.

Porteguee Frank removed the specially ordered Bowie knife mailed to him from New Orleans, Louisiana. He also spun it while he knelt to cut off the proof of his successful hunt and kills.

Porteguee Frank Morales left his three victims lying in the grass, minus their six ears. He whistled a tune, and he and his horse lazily rode away.

The next day, Porteguee Frank sat on the porch and handed the rancher proof of his completed contract. The old man smiled, lifted what was surely a woman's ear, and yelled into the bloody remains.

"Apodrecer no inferno!"

"All three will be rotting in hell, Señor," Frank said, not in the least disturbed by the old rancher's tactless anger at the rustlers he had killed.

The old man tossed the ear into the dirt at the front of his wide porch, and several dogs fought for it. He held up his glass of wine and toasted Frank. After he drank, he threw a bag at the bounty hunter. By the weight, the amount inside was correct. Frank had done the work so often; he knew the bag contained his promised six hundred dollars in gold. He started to rise from his chair, when the old rancher placed a hand on his shoulder, reached into his coat, and brought out a bright red envelope.

"While you were performing your duty for me, this arrived by courier from Rio. Perhaps it is important."

Frank sat back onto the seat and looked over the strange envelope. He broke the wax seal and read, lowered the invitation, and then brought it back up and read again.

"Another employment opportunity?" the old rancher asked.

Porteguee Frank placed the red letter inside his vest and jingled the small leather bag of gold.

"An opportunity has arisen in America."

"Ah, another hunt perhaps?"

Frank stood and pocketed his money, knowing he would need all he had.

"Possibly much more than that." Frank stepped off the porch and smiled. He hefted himself into the saddle after inspecting the brand-new Henry repeating rifle, with the long telescopic glass scope ensconced in its scabbard.

On his way to the port of Rio, he had thoughts of his own penny dreadful and the fame the book would possibly bring him. Now young men could try and emulate *his* deeds.

His thoughts turned to the distant and wild land of Wyoming and the handsome reward for a hunt he knew he was capable of fulfilling.

WASHINGTON, D.C.

The Fourth Invitee

The Harvard Room at the Continental Hotel was full, packed with mostly brass from the war department. The civilians watched in awe. Men they had read about in newspapers for their exploits during the war roamed, smoked cigars, and drank the night away. A lone table had been curtained off for a special guest of the dining room staff that night. This man desired very little attention and often ate with only two men, outside of his dinners with his wife and son in their home. The man sat and drank whiskey, smoked cigars, and silently listened to his two subordinates voicing their current problems.

The new general of the army—a posting created especially for him by Congress—Ulysses S. Grant watched the two men argue seemingly for his benefit. Finally, Grant slapped a white-gloved hand hard onto the table. Both generals, William Tecumseh Sherman and Philip H. Sheridan, stopped their argument and looked at their commander.

"You are both arguing a matter and subject you know I despise. If you put George Custer at the head of that damned command, the man will end up raiding villages and killing women and children in their sleep. You know that, and you both still argue for his appointment!"

"Who but Custer could lead the Seventh?" Sheridan asked, waving away the smoke from Grant's cigar.

Grant picked up a small bell and rang it. Soon his adjutant stepped through the red curtain. The general only had to nod his head and the man left.

"I have another in mind." Grant lifted his crystal glass and downed the whiskey it held.

An officer wearing the silver eagles of a full colonel entered the small, enclosed area. Both Sherman and Sheridan became immediately apprehensive. The officer stood at attention before the three most powerful soldiers in the world.

"Colonel Jackson reporting as ordered, General." The man saluted.

"Knock off the bullshit and sit your ass down, John." Grant ordered the uniformed waiter to fill his glass and that of another. He slid the second over to the newly arrived officer as he sat down. "Phil, Bill, you both know Colonel Jackson?"

"You know damn good and well we know him, Sam. In fact, we both wanted him to take command of the newly formed Seventh Cavalry, but he turned us down flat," Sheridan said sharply with a hard glance at Jackson.

"Well, that was you. Now *I'm* asking."

Grant turned and faced Colonel John Calhoun Jackson, a man trained by one of the greatest cavalry commanders in the nation's history—General John Buford, the hero of Gettysburg. And even before the first shots of the war were fired, Jackson had also been offered a job as a Corp Commander under Stonewall Jackson in the recent rebellion, by none other than Confederate President Jefferson Davis. But before the first shots of the war were fired at Fort Sumter, Jackson had decided to go with General Buford's new division of cavalry.

"John, I know you're anxious to get back to that wasteland you call a state, but I'm offering you the command of the newly formed Seventh Cavalry at Fort Riley, Kansas. You're a Texan, one that's maybe not too welcome back home. But you know the territory from Texas and Kansas to Dakota and Montana. You damn well know Indians. I need you out there. We have an especially bad problem near Fort Kearny. It seems a crazed Sioux warrior is on a rampage from Nebraska to Montana. I suspect, with your background, you've heard of him—Running Horse. If he ever teams up with that new Indian kid, Crazy Horse, there will be hell to pay out there."

"No one knows much about him," Jackson said. "He stays clear of whites altogether. But rampaging is not his style. That man has a reason for all he does."

"Well, word out of Fort Laramie is that the 'skin's family was massacred by settlers and he's on a vengeance run," Phil Sheridan said.

"This happened in Dakota Territory?" Jackson asked.

"Somewhere north of the Little Bighorn River."

"Now you see. This is why we need you to command the Seventh in Kansas." Grant puffed his cigar back to life.

With the thought of a man like Running Horse on the rampage, the offer wasn't as good as Grant made out.

"General, I'm grateful for both your offer and the general's here. But my family needs me back home. My army days are done. I'm going to have a hard enough time not getting shot by family and neighbors for joining the wrong side. And if great warriors like Running Horse are pushed into fighting, the killing could go on for years. I just can't do it."

"Told you, Sam. The boy's not interested. We have to go with our second option." Sherman sipped his coffee.

"John, you said it yourself: Your family won't be too welcoming when you get home. As you just stated, your pa is quite put out because he believes you fought on the wrong side."

The colonel looked at Grant and slowly nodded in agreement. He took the drink in front of him and downed it quickly.

"We have a real Indian problem heading our way. I need you to talk some sense into them for me. If not, these two humanists here, with stars on their shoulder boards, would prefer to wipe them off the face of the earth. You're the best scout and tracker that this nation's army has ever produced, in my opinion. I need you to take command of that new cavalry unit."

"We have to solve this problem once and for all," Sherman said. "The sooner we handle it, the sooner we can get onto the business of taming this continent." His remark was directed at Grant. He was referring to making a fast, strike-first blow against the Northern Plain's tribes, and that assault should be delivered by a proven killer—Custer.

"You see, John, the only friend the Indians will have is you. The man *they* want will use the opportunity to climb up the army ladder any way he can."

The colonel probably had an idea who Grant was referring to but seemed to want confirmation. "Who is that?" Jackson asked, holding out his glass for a refill.

"We want Custer since you're resigning your commission," Sheridan answered.

Jackson again swallowed his whiskey. He placed the glass down a little harder than he had to.

"Well?" Grant said.

"What do you want me to say? That the arrogant bastard is a glory seeker that cares nothing for his men? Hell, I would respect him more if he hated the men he fought against. Instead, he uses them as a possible headline in the newspapers. I know your reservations about Custer, General, and I wholeheartedly agree. He'll get his headlines eventually, I guarantee it, just not in the way he thinks. The warriors he'll be facing won't be worn-out Southerners with little fight left in 'em. They're angry, General. And to tell you the truth, they have a right to be. I want nothing to do with their eventual destruction. What will happen to them is inevitable, but I want nothing to do with it. I've done enough for king and country. I want no more killing in my life."

Grant lowered his head in defeat. He nodded his acceptance of the colonel's right to be free of slaughter because, god only knew, he felt the same way.

"So, you're heading back to Texas, then?"

"Yes, sir."

"Broke as hell, I suspect, from sending your army pay back to folks that despise you?"

Jackson smiled at the correctness and bluntness of General Grant.

"I have enough to get by."

The general again raised the bell and jingled it. The adjutant arrived shortly.

"Give the colonel the letter that arrived at the War Department last month while he was in Charleston."

The major vanished and soon returned with a bright red envelope. He handed it to the colonel. "General, excuse me, but Lieutenant Colonel Custer is waiting in the dining room."

"Ask the colonel to join us," Grant said with a frown. He looked at both Sheridan and Sherman. "Satisfied?"

The men said nothing. Grant was in no mood after being turned down by a man he respected more than any other officer in the disbanded Army of the Potomac.

Colonel John C. Jackson turned the bright red envelope over in his hands and examined the seal. It was already broken, which meant it had previously been read. Grant smiled for the first time that evening.

"Looks like I've been caught at it. Yes, I read it. I'm a damn general. I can do anything I want. Besides, I wanted to know about my possible competition for your services. Can't blame me. That's one hell of an offer in there." Grant blew out a cloud of cigar smoke.

Jackson read the letter and looked at Grant.

"It would surely alleviate your money problem, whatever the hell this contest is. What would an ancient predator be? And one that is of pure white pelt?"

"General," Jackson said and stood. He nodded at Sherman and Sheridan.

"Still heading to Texas?" Grant took a drink of his whiskey.

Colonel Jackson didn't reply. He started to leave the small room, when the curtain opened and a man with a mustache, goatee, and freshly trimmed reddish-blond hair entered. The man was much smaller in stature than Jackson, but his bearing said, at the very least, he thought himself far superior.

"George," Jackson said with a disdainful smirk.

"John," Custer replied in return. "And it's General Custer, Colonel."

Jackson smiled at the arrogance of the smaller man. "No, George, I believe you're paid at the rank of lieutenant colonel since the war ended your brevet status, the same as myself." Jackson started to turn and leave but stopped and faced the man from Michigan "Hm, I'm guessing that means, as a full colonel, I still outrank you, doesn't it? And the wonder of it all, Armstrong, is the fact the world still turns on its axis."

Grant almost spit out the whiskey he had in his bearded cheeks while he watched his friend leave.

"That is the most ill-mannered officer I have ever encountered." Custer faced the three generals. He looked at Grant. "Where's he off to, Texas?"

"No, I believe he may head northwest of there. Cheyenne, I think. He's going to test his tracking skills for something other than killing his fellow man."

BRITISH RAJ FORCES
PUNJAB PROVINCE, INDIA

The Fifth Invitee

They were surrounded. The young lieutenant's company, part of the world-famous Tenth Bengal Lancers, had been ordered to track down and stop the murdering bandit chieftain, Suliman

Khan, before he and his small army could escape back into his stronghold near the mountainous terrain of the Hindu Kush.

Lieutenant Alfred Simpson had been ordered to track but not engage his quarry until a regional expert who had a deep understanding of the bandit chieftain was brought in. But Simpson had seen little reason to await a Sikh mystic with questionable allegiances. Now, through his arrogance, he and his 112 men would die before the sun rose the next day.

The small depression in the red earth was just large enough to keep bandit sharpshooters from getting a clear shot at them. But the frightened Simpson knew, when it was close to dawn, Suliman Khan would send his full force of three hundred men in to massacre them all. He passed out the last of their water supply.

The Indian sentry shouted from his hidden spot behind an outcropping of jagged rock.

"Horseman coming in, Sahib!"

"Only one?" Simpson asked his color sergeant, a burly man with a black beard who had his arm bandaged and in a sling.

"I don't believe our courier made the run to Punjab, sir. I don't think any assistance in force is coming."

The young lieutenant's face and body deflated. The larger man slapped the boy on the shoulder.

"No worries, sir. The Lancers have been in tighter spots before this."

Lieutenant Simpson half-heartedly smiled, knowing the color sergeant was lying for the benefit of the men and himself. He huffed out his chest and turned when the rider approached.

Shots rang out from the surrounding hills, and each echoed across the barren landscape. Both horse and rider swerved first one way and then the next. Bullets struck all around the rider, but none found their mark. The man might have been a fool, but he was a brave one. The horse jumped the steep wall of rock and sand, making the last fifty feet into the camp of besieged men. The rider launched free of the saddle before the horse slid to a stop.

Lieutenant Simpson was amazed by the turban and red sash over the man's black hair. He was a Sikh. And the most amazing thing about the man's appearance was his uniform. Not only was it a British officer's uniform, but one that also had the insignia of a British army captain.

The man straightened his tunic and adjusted his chest strap, the Webley pistol in its flapped holster. The beard was thick but well-trimmed. He walked right up to the sergeant and the lieutenant.

"Is this all the help we will receive?" an angry Simpson asked.

The man in the white Dastar turban said nothing.

The color sergeant nudged the arm of the young lieutenant and brought his own hand up in a proper salute. After a moment's confusion, Simpson followed suit.

The man with the black beard hesitated before returning the gesture of military respect.

"Sorry, Captain, I have never seen a Sikh officer before this day."

"Obviously not, Lieutenant." The captain looked around at the defensive measures Simpson had ordered. He shook his head. "Color Sergeant, why is there a roaring fire, where the men are but highlighted targets for sharpshooters?"

"The men were cold and hungry. That's—"

The captain held up his hand at Simpson. The man closed his mouth.

"It was my order, sir," the color sergeant said.

"Not a good way to start out, Color Sergeant, lying to your new commander. Now, douse that fire before someone gets themselves seriously hurt." His dark, accusing eyes went to the young, brash lieutenant.

"Sir!" the color sergeant said, hurrying off.

"Why not feed and warm the men if we are to be left out here to be slaughtered?" Simpson said while the captain looked at him. "Sir," Simpson finally added but not with much respect.

"You seem unusually depressed by the situation you have gotten your men into, Lieutenant. You should be. You exceeded your orders quite substantially. You were supposed to track Suliman Khan and then inform command of his whereabouts. Nothing more. Instead, you tried to become a hero of the British Raj by attacking in an unfriendly territory and without knowing the disposition of your enemy." The captain looked up at the mountains. He sniffed, smelling the air, and walked away.

"Look, Captain, there's a lot of bloody bandits out there. We are surrounded, sir. Maybe as many as two or three hundred."

Captain Ranjit Singh stopped his walk, turned, and took in the lieutenant's fearful face. The moonlight highlighted the boy's complete terror of dying.

"You seem easily impressed by numbers, Lieutenant." The captain started unraveling his Dastar. He went to his knees, and his hip-length black hair tumbled free. Singh prayed, stood, and handed the color sergeant the long ribbon of his Dastar. "Mind this for me, Color Sergeant."

"Sir!"

"What are you doing?" Simpson asked.

The Sikh unfastened his chest strap belt and holster and handed those to the color sergeant as well. He unbuttoned his tunic and removed the white blouse underneath, exposing his brown skin to the moonlight. When the color sergeant turned to leave, Singh stopped him and pulled free the large knife from the scabbard on his belt. He nodded the sergeant away.

"Captain, may I ask what your plan is?"

The Oxford and Sandhurst Academy–educated Ranjit Singh faced the blond-haired Englishman. "Why, I'm going to attempt to alleviate the mess you have created, Lieutenant Simpson."

"With just a knife and no men?"

"If I fail in my duty this night, Lieutenant—which means that, yes, indeed, you and the men will be massacred—go to your God in heaven with my advice ringing in your arrogant ears, boy. When in doubt, if at all possible, destroy an enemy's will to fight. This"—he held up the shiny knife—"is my solution to checkmate. Don't change the chess pieces on the board. Change the rules."

Lieutenant Simpson was confused, but he watched Captain Singh run off into the setting moon.

The sun rose slowly over the mountain range of the far-off Hindu Kush. Lieutenant Simpson watched the 250 bandits of the warlord Suliman Khan ease onto the plain to their front. He removed his pith helmet and wiped sweat from the headband. Simpson glanced at his brave color sergeant. He had his whistle planted in his lips and his small, rounded club he used to frighten recruits tucked under his red-coated arm.

The color sergeant looked at the circle of 112 men lying prone inside the depression. They had their Model 1865 Remington rolling block rifles aimed outward, bravely facing their destiny at the hands of the ruthless Suliman Khan.

Lieutenant Simpson swallowed his fear and replaced his helmet. He slowly withdrew his saber.

"Steady boys, steady. Let's take as many of the bastards with us as we can." Simpson stepped to the top of the small ridge and planted his sword in the earth, making as proud a pose for his men as he could while facing the moving line of bandits. He only wished he could have witnessed the death of the arrogant Sikh captain before he met his maker.

The long front line of Suliman Khan's men stopped. Horses whinnied and a few reared, readying the charge.

All the men in the defensive depression were shocked when the far left of the line turned about, quickly followed by the center and the far right. The bandits brought their horses to a gallop, exiting the field without firing a shot.

Dust and the sounds from the running horses was brought in by the morning wind while the bandits simply rode away. Another freshening breeze cleared the area to their front. The men stood, unable to fathom what they were witnessing.

"I'll be bloody goddamned!" the bearded color sergeant said. He held up his unbroken arm in a cheer.

Simpson couldn't believe his eyes.

Standing in what would have been the rear of the bandit line of charge was Captain Ranjit Singh. He was there, bare-chested, with long black hair and beard blowing in the wind, holding a long staff. The head of the bandit leader, Suliman Khan, was pegged to the staff's sharpened end. The hair was moving out from the decapitated head.

"I always heard it but never believed it," the color sergeant said when Simpson joined him.

The men cheered louder at their sudden reprieve from slaughter.

"How?" was all Simpson could utter.

"If the man that kills a leader is worthy, that man becomes the new leader. He simply snuck into their camp, killed the Khan, and then just ordered the bandits to go home." The large man shook his head in wonder. "Bloody amazing."

An hour later, Ranjit Singh was getting his uniform on. The grateful men of the company smiled and praised the Sikh for his skill at command. Simpson, of course, was not one of these. He stood aloof while Singh received the praise of *his* men.

It wasn't long before they heard the bugle calls of the arriving relief force—five hours late, but the men were thankful to have another company of cavalry. The leading officer, also a captain of the Ninth British Fusiliers, bypassed the young lieutenant and rode straight up to Captain Singh. He saluted and hopped down from his horse. The men from both companies stared at the Sikh who had saved the beleaguered force.

"Captain Singh, compliments of Colonel Diedrickson, sir." The captain saluted his equal out of respect.

Singh returned the salute and tied off his Dastar. "Glad you could join us, Captain. I'm afraid you rode all this way for nothing. I believe the problem regarding Suliman Khan has been resolved."

The captain looked momentarily confused.

"That's not why we are here, Captain Singh. The colonel has sent you a communique from London through Delhi." The captain clicked his heels together and offered Singh a red letter of strange design.

Singh looked from the letter to the captain.

"I believe whoever sent it has a bit of bluster, sir. It was forwarded through the House of Lords to the viceroy in Delhi. I am to report to you that your ship leaves in three days."

Singh walked off and read the invitation.

"I have no wish to do this thing." Singh tried to hand the red letter back to the captain, who took a step back as if the letter had plague germs on it.

"Captain, the colonel said you may have that reaction." The captain rummaged in his red tunic and brought out another regular-sized envelope.

Singh just looked at him.

"As I said, sir, whoever forwarded the letter to you has a bit of clout, he does. These are orders from Parliament in London. You are to leave immediately."

Singh walked off with his new orders in his hand. The captain climbed on top of his horse and ordered his men to follow suit. He eased his mount over to where Singh stood staring at the mountains of his homeland. The captain cleared his throat until Singh looked up.

"If you don't mind me asking, Captain Singh, what is all of this about?"

"I have orders for America."

"The bleedin' States? What in the bloody hell for, sir?"

Singh gazed at the mountains once more.

"It seems I am now involved in a contest of sorts."

"Ah, but command has surely gone mad." The captain turned his horse away and left the camp with his men behind him.

Captain Ranjit Singh just stared at the mountains of the Hindu Kush, knowing in his heart he would never see them again.

OSAKA, JAPAN

The Sixth Invitee

Oishi Takanawa sat on the cold, cobbled floor of the Palace of the Cherry Blossoms. His chains restrained him from reaching the water bowl only three feet from him. He stared at the liquid. His stamina was running far short of the energy he would need to finish his punishment. The rotted meat wasn't as tempting to him as the water needed. Oishi would be facing his most challenging opponent in the next death match and suspected his thirst would soon be a distant memory of his life.

He thought back on his crime against Miyouri Shinzou, the most powerful warlord and samurai in Osaka—killing of the master's chief council. The warlord was a man of low morals who had been caught stealing and murdering without the permission of the great samurai from Takanawa's village. The brute had killed two children and their mother in arrogance, which dictated his death. The villagers were tired of the way they were treated by the great samurai and his council.

The real crime of Takanawa's deed, although proper in his eyes, was handing out justice without the permission of his master. As a result, instead of being killed outright, his sentence was to survive ten battles against the most accomplished warriors of the region, as a self-trained master of the sword and the rifle in his own right.

After the ten straight victories, the local villagers and most of the samurai's council had shifted their allegiance and fully backed his achievement as something that would be turned into legend. They grumbled that their village's hero would have to face another ten when the first had been dispatched in quick order. This fact infuriated the great samurai, who felt a loss of control. With wounds that would have sent a lesser warrior to his great rest, Takanawa had fought with a serious gash to his chest, crisscrossing down to his left hip.

But the lack of water would be his eventual undoing.

Takanawa closed his eyes and awaited his next challenge, knowing whatever was chosen, he would fail. The lack of food and water had been his greatest enemy, and that enemy always won in the end.

Samurai Master Miyouri Shinzou sat cross-legged on the bamboo mat, deep in thought. His chief council, a squirrel of a man, was positioned across from him with a scroll. The names were of every man in the local village calling for the release of the warrior, Takanawa. The samurai was in a popular bind he saw no escape from. Was his word stronger than the wishes of the people he protected? Or was his rule being challenged by the peasant who lived in the small village his foolish aide had sought murder in?

Shinzou was cornered. If he finished off the small warrior, he would encounter a possible uprising. He would also lose face with the new, young emperor in Tokyo.

"Perhaps we need to take the question out of our purview, my lord," said the smaller man.

"I know not your meaning," Shinzou replied.

"Your fame as a warrior has spread far and wide. The newspapers in Europe write of your exploits as if they were mere adventure tales. Let us use this. If my plan is successful, you solve two problems at one time, great one."

"And how do I accomplish this thing?"

"The people love and respect the peasant for his action to protect them, is this not true?"

"Obviously."

"But for his deed, you have placed yourself into the corner of a flooding room. You accused him and have set punishment before you knew the desires of the villagers. Now, if you follow through on his execution, you not only lose the faith of your people, but you may anger the new emperor, who is just a boy, subject to the tales of great warriors such as Takanawa. Is this not so?"

The samurai wasn't following his advisor's logic. He shook his head.

"My lord, the solution is in the fact that you can no longer kill your prisoner without losing the following of your people and attracting the attention of a mere boy who sits on the throne. So, we eliminate one or the other."

"You talk treason. I cannot remove the emperor!"

"Not at all, my lord. But you can eliminate Takanawa and not kill him overtly in the process."

"The days of magic have long since passed, old one. How can this be done?"

The older man reached into his garish yellow gown and produced a bright red letter with a ribbon and wax seal on it. "This is an offer from Europe. It was supposed to be yours. You cannot accept the proposition it announces, but someone from your prefecture can. This will solve your problems. Eliminate Takanawa and ease the minds of the people. The emperor will never be the wiser."

The samurai held out his hand and took the red invitation.

The door opened, and a fresh pail of water and a large bowl of rice and meat was brought in. The guards, who quickly unlocked the manacles from Takanawa's wrists, even provided a lantern. A small man who was a local physician was escorted in. He examined Takanawa's deep wounds. The physician declared Takanawa would live and that he would be back to stitch up the battle injuries.

Takanawa wasn't really confused. The new treatment was a way of telling him the punishment of challenges by other warriors was at an end. He would be fed, watered, and then decapitated. At least it would be a more sensible and humane death. It was that simple. His warlord master was not the sort to commute a sentence. His rule over the small villages of his prefecture had been absolute for years.

The guards left. What was strange, as Takanawa slurped the cold water greedily, was the fact the door of the cell remained wide open. He lifted rice to his mouth. The guards outside scrambled away, and Takanawa prepared himself for his execution. He set the bowl of rice and meat aside and slowly, painfully stood. Footsteps drew near.

The warlord, Samurai Master Miyouri Shinzou, stood with hands on hips. His sword hung from his sash. His hair was done in a traditional topknot, and his clothing was silk of the brightest red. Shinzou stood looking at the man who had taken the job of judge, jury, and executioner into his own hands, had insulted the samurai, and had usurped his power over his people.

"The village healer has attended you?"

"As much as a dead man needs, yes." Takanawa bowed his respect to Shinzou.

The samurai entered the cell. He wrinkled his nose at the smell but kept his composure at the way the great warrior peasant had been treated. Shinzou had thought Takanawa was secured in comfortable quarters. This bad fate had been meted out by his council behind his back. Now Shinzou understood why the local villagers of his prefecture were in an uproarious and rebellious mood lately. He would have to make adjustments. But one problem at a time.

He withdrew the samurai sword from its scabbard and held it out. Takanawa lowered his neck, accepting his fate. When no killing blow came, Takanawa looked up. The sword was being offered to him. The great samurai moved his own head in a bow.

"If you seek justice for your ill treatment, I will offer no resistance."

"I seek no revenge against you, my lord. But I do seek justice for my people." Takanawa stumbled forward, trying to keep the pain of his wounds to a minimum. "I did what I did because word would have been returned to you by your council that what your man did in my village was a response to some form of disrespect to him. He would have claimed justification in his act of murder and returned here with no punishment given."

"Has my rule been usurped that bad in my villages that you no longer trust your lord for justice?"

Takanawa looked closely at the older man. He lowered his head, unable to speak the truth to someone with little patience for that small requirement of a ruler of men. Takanawa relaxed when the sword returned to the samurai's scabbard.

"The punishment for the crime of willing vigilante justice is, of course, death. This I can no longer do and call it justice. Now my difficulty, Takanawa-san. You must vanish from this place."

"I am to be banished?" the young peasant asked.

"In a sense, yes. I have a task for you. You have become a great warrior over the few years that you have lived. I am sending you as my representative to America. You will be taught their ways and learn all that my scholars know about the barbarians in the West."

"What is the task?" Takanawa asked.

The samurai brought out the letter. The invitation was done in expert Japanese writing. He handed it to Takanawa.

"You will be issued the finest weapons of your choosing made specially from my private armory. You will not only be representing me and the prefecture, but word will spread to Tokyo and the new emperor. All of Japan will know you for what you are, Takanawa-san—the greatest self-trained samurai in all of Japan."

"But I am no samurai." Takanawa bowed his head.

"As of now, I declare you as such. The people will know you as such. Our prayers go with you."

The samurai bowed and quickly exited, leaving Takanawa stunned. The samurai sword remained leaning against the cell wall. Miyouri Shinzou had left him his personal sword.

Takanawa looked from the sword to the red letter he held in his hand. After the words it had said, Japan would be forever a thing of his past. His lord and master had found a new and inventive way to kill him.

Takanawa was off to America and the barbaric West.

CLAY COUNTY, MISSOURI

The Seventh and Final Invitee

Smithville was one of those towns time had passed by. With most of the male population either dead or in deep debt to the federal government for back taxes not paid during the recent rebellion, it seemed the small burg couldn't hold on for much longer.

The man rode slowly through town. Women stared and suddenly pulled their small children from the dirt street. He was a sight not fit for townsfolk, but after a full year in a federal prison camp, his beard and ragged uniform were all he had. His horse had been donated to him by a discharged Union officer who admired his conduct during the war years.

The big man reined his horse over to the office of the town's marshal. Before stepping from the McClellan saddle, he used his right hand to tip his battered hat at a young woman. The woman scurried past, ignoring his etiquette as if he were a spook from some haunted story of her childhood.

When he stepped from the tired roan, he stumbled, still weak from his year of captivity. The spot on his shoulders where his Confederate rank used to be was darker in color than the faded gray coat. The only way anyone could tell he had been an officer was the white stripe down his pant legs. The dingy white shirt was from the officer's quarters in New York, where he had been discharged and released into the world after the surrender of Robert E. Lee in Virginia.

He stepped onto the wooden boardwalk and stomped his knee-high boots, trying to get feeling back into his legs after his long journey from New York to Missouri. The man removed his hat and wiped his sweating forehead. His long black hair fell free from where the hat had contained the strands. He reached for the door handle and opened it.

The man stood at the door, allowing his eyes to adjust to the darkness. There was movement in the back, and a figure veiled in early morning glare exited the small cell area. He remained easy while the man stopped and took in the ragged visitor.

"What can I do ya for, stranger?" The heavyset man went to a stove and poured himself a tin cup of coffee.

"I know I must be a sight, but calling me a stranger hurts my feelings a bit, John."

The man turned at the sound of the voice with the familiar ring to it. He studied the visitor, and a smile slowly crossed his whisker-stubbled face.

"Kyle? Kyle Freemantle, that you?" He set the coffee down and held out his hand.

Freemantle took the offered gesture and shook with as much authority as he could. He found out quickly the strong grip of years past wasn't there any longer. Freemantle quickly released the hand of Marshal John Pierce.

"I can't believe you made it out alive, Kyle boy. You wouldn't believe the rumors we heard after Gettysburg. Wasn't soon after that the Yank and Southern newspaper boys lost track of you."

"Ran into a little trouble chasing down old Phil Sheridan in the Shenandoah Valley. Been a mite cooped up since."

The marshal looked him over and then hurriedly handed him the coffee. "Here, Kyle. You look like you need this more than me."

Freemantle placed his hat on the marshal's desk and gratefully accepted the cup.

"That's coffee too, not chicory. Coffee's been comin' through regular since the carpetbaggers came around. Yanks can't do without their foofaraw."

Freemantle sipped the glorious coffee and savored it. He closed his eyes and, in doing so, brought on visions of better days, when his family had a prosperous farm and horses by the hundreds. Freemantle smiled at the marshal when he opened his eyes.

"Carpetbaggers abundant, are they?"

The marshal grew quiet. The question disturbed the old man. Instead of answering, Pierce went to his desk and brought out a brown bottle. He poured some of the clear liquid into the coffee cup and did the same to a fresh mug he retrieved from the stove.

Freemantle noticed the discomfort of his old friend and sat on the edge of the desk.

"How's the homeplace? Pa doin' all right?"

The marshal sat in the swivel chair and took a long pull of the coffee laced with the liquor. He looked away.

"John?" Freemantle persisted.

"Your pa's dead, Kyle. Been dead goin' on eight months now."

Kyle Freemantle placed the cup down and looked at the overweight marshal. He didn't push. Freemantle waited, as was his way.

After another deep pull of the liquor, the marshal stood and looked out the window. He spoke with his back to the former Confederate major. "He put up a fight when the carpetbaggers put your place up for auction. Back taxes, they say. You know your pa, Kyle. He didn't take kindly to Yankees comin' down here and stealin' from folk." Pierce turned and watched Freemantle finish his coffee, dark eyes made even darker by the beard and sun-wrinkled face.

"Livestock?" Freemantle closed his eyes, choking back emotions he had thought were lost on the battlefield and among the years of death he had endured.

"Horses were confiscated. That's the Yankee way of sayin' 'legally stolen.'"

"Were you there, John?"

"I was. I couldn't talk your pa into livin' after they took it all. You know him. He was never one to bluff."

Freemantle stood. His legs seemed less shaky, and his will had slowly returned.

"Where are you goin', Kyle? What now?"

Freemantle slowly placed the battered white hat on his head without facing the marshal. He turned to leave.

"The house and barn is still up. No one's taken possession of the property yet. The bank will let you stay until you get on your feet. I'll see to it."

Freemantle stopped by the front door. "That's not home no more, John. Pa was what made it home. Not wood and nails. If I may ask, Marshal, how did you let my pa get shot down by a bunch of invaders?"

"Kyle, it was all legal. Wasn't much I could do—"

The marshal was talking to an empty space. Freemantle left before he heard his answer.

Former Major Kyle Freemantle of the Army of Northern Virginia placed his last dollar on the table. The bartender took away the empty bottle. Freemantle's hat hid the fury in his eyes. A group of loud men laughed in the far corner of the barroom, but he paid them no mind.

"Like this fella here," a voice said. "Gone and run off to fight with the so-called real army while the homefolk suffered at the hands of Kansas Redleg's militia and Yankee soldiers out for plunder. Hell, we did more Yankee killin' with 'Bloody Bill' Anderson and Billy Quantrill than they did with old Bobby Lee, runnin' around up North like they did!"

"Shut up, Jesse, and sit down," another voice said.

Freemantle sat unmoving while the distant voices talked on.

His mind was on the last time he had seen his father and the ranch hands they supported. Everyone had gathered to say goodbye to the boy going off to fight the real war. He was disturbed that he couldn't remember his father's face. Every time Freemantle tried, it was like looking at a doll whose features and button eyes hadn't been stitched on yet.

"Hell, men like that ragamuffin over there run out on friends and family when they were needed right here at home. Instead, they go off and try to get their names in Northern newspapers. Ain't that right?"

"Now look, are we here to talk business or listen to your brother shoot off that mouth of his?"

"My little brother can do most anything he wants, Cole, and you know that."

"Well, if he keeps on like this, he's apt to get his ass whooped. Do you know who that fella is, Frank?" the larger man asked, lowering his voice.

"How should I know? I figured I wouldn't be able to tell until he scraped some of that road dirt from his face."

"Frank, that's Kyle Freemantle. All my life, I grew up hearin' 'bout him. He don't take much guff. I would tell Jesse to let him be."

There was a laugh, and a chair scraped on the wooden floor as it was moved. Still, Freemantle's eyes remained down. He placed his hands on the faded green felt table and longed for another drink.

"Is that right, Ragamuffin? You a war hero?"

Although Kyle Freemantle sensed the presence near him, he kept his eyes fixed on the table.

"We needed all our kinfolk here, not off fightin' in Virginia. Tell me, where did that get ya?"

"That's enough, Jesse," the same voice as before said from the far corner. "He don't mean nothin' by it, Freemantle. He's just full of sour oats."

"Shut up, Cole Younger, or I'll set my sights toward you! That'd end this new partnership real quick, wouldn't it?"

"Go on, then. Tell this man how you really feel. I wanna see this," the long-haired balding man said from his chair.

Freemantle's hat was pulled off and thrown onto the table.

"Now, why don't you head on out of here, officer." The young man laughed at his fellows in the far corner of the room. "A'fore, I show you how we do it in Missouri."

"I ain't heeled, boy. Go on now, before something bad happens." Freemantle didn't bother looking into the steely eyes of the twenty-year-old Jesse James.

"Oh, we can get you a pistol, old man." James crooked a smile at the table full of friends. "Show us how the cavalry did it. Then I'll demonstrate to these fine folks the ways of the new South."

Freemantle slowly stood and took the hat from the table. "Don't need no pistol to get over on the likes of you, boy. Now, I said to get before you really knock over the beehive."

Jesse James stepped back, going for the pistol on his chest in a crossover holster and strap. Freemantle stopped James's hand from moving by pinning it to his sternum. With his fingers tantalizingly close to the draw, Jesse looked up and into the darkest eyes he had ever seen. The stranger removed the pistol and tossed it to the floor, then brought his filthy white hat up and started to slap James with the brim mercilessly.

Jesse's face went numb from the blows of the thickened felt hat. "You fight fair, old man!"

Still, the blows from the hat rained on the smaller man. Finally, Jesse James crashed to the floor with tears in his eyes. His big brother, Frank, stood and went for his gun. Cole Younger reached his first.

"The war be over, Frank. Maybe you had better explain that to your little brother. We don't start a partnership by shootin' unarmed Southerners."

"Not a good way to start, Cole." Frank looked sideways at the man holding a gun on him.

"Yeah, but Jesse needs to know when too much is too much. It'll get us into trouble someday."

Frank James lowered his gun and hesitantly holstered it. Cole Younger retrieved the pistol that had been knocked from the young killer's hand. He shoved it into his belt.

"Give me back my gun!" Jesse slowly rose from the floor with his bloody nose and lips.

"When we be five miles down the road, maybe. But not now."

"What goes on here?"

The barroom quieted as the men at the table noticed the gruff marshal standing in their midst.

"Why, Marshal, we was just leavin'. Ain't that right, Frank?" Cole Younger winked at Freemantle.

Frank pushed an infuriated Jesse toward the door of the saloon. "As he said, we were just leavin', Marshal." He gave a glare toward Kyle Freemantle.

Jesse was a little harder to control. They walked out with the Younger clan not far behind.

Freemantle returned to his chair and sat. He placed his hat back on and lowered his eyes again. Something heavy landed on the table—an old Navy Colt revolving pistol and the holster, with six extra cylinders of cap and ball ammunition. There was also his father's Henry repeater with a box of 44.40 shells.

"Thought you might be needin' those, with all of the

high-class folk we have roamin' the town. I guess you just met a few of 'em." The marshal pulled out a chair and sat, uninvited.

"I know Cole. He was a big idiot back then and still looks to be. But he's never been stupid. If he's mixin' up with Frank and that little brother of his, that proves my point." Freemantle glanced at the marshal. "What do you want, John?"

"You left in a huff before I could tell you." The marshal produced a small leather bag and tossed it onto the table. "'T'ain't much, but it's all I have. You take it and leave, Kyle boy. Ain't nothin' here for you anymore."

Freemantle pushed the bag back to the marshal. "I'll get by. 'Sides, where in the hell am I to go? Lie to the federals and get myself a new name, like Smith or Jones, and join the army?"

"And fight Injuns? I don't see that. You were never a killer for no reason, just the most skilled man with a long rifle I have ever seen. I s'pose your skill there hasn't been lost."

"John, stop greasin' the pig and tell me what it is you want."

"You also left before I could give you this." The marshal tossed a large, battered red envelope on the table next to the bag of money. "The Pinkerton bastards delivered it 'bout the same time your pa was killed. I read it. It may be an answer you're lookin' for, or it may not. Anyway, Kyle boy, I gave you my last forty dollars and a way to defend yourself. It's up to you what you do. If you stay here, you'll more'n likely fall in with boys like the Jameses and Youngers. My advice is to get while the gettin's good." He stood and left the money, weapons, and letter on the table.

An hour later, after half a bottle of whiskey, Kyle Freemantle finally laid the red-letter invitation on the table. He fingered the old Navy Colt in its holster and closed his eyes in thought. His life here in Clay County was over. He had more than likely known it the day he saddled his horse up in 1861.

Was it the fact he always knew farm and ranching life was never meant for him? Was he ready to come to terms with the fact he *was* a killer and always would be? His old cavalry commander, J.E.B. Stuart, had said he was the most natural tracker he had ever seen. The Northern newspapers had written about his exploits more than a dozen times. Freemantle never believed the tales told of himself. But the papers weren't far from the truth.

He stood, pocketed the bag of money, and placed the belt and holster on his hip. Freemantle took the rifle and shells, left the saloon in Smithville, Clay County, Missouri, for the last time, and started down the long road to Cheyenne, Wyoming.

CHAPTER TWO

BALTIMORE, MARYLAND

Vladimir Alexandros leaned on his diamond-tipped cane and looked off into the foggy Maryland night. The carriage was of the gilded variety and appropriate to the way the Rumanian lord's special assistant liked to travel. The night was muggy and humid, but in insecure deference, he kept the carriage windows up. His small bowler hat was perched jauntily on his head while he waited.

The hired coachman sat atop and wondered why his charge kept such a distance between himself and the cargo the hired wagon parked behind them was there to receive.

Alexandros's gloved hand tickled the trigger of a Webley six-shot pistol inside his coat. The last of the crates was offloaded. The weapon was a precaution, just in case his employer's second shipment to the New World had broken free of their confinement. Until the six crates were secure, the recently arrived man from Rumania via France would be overly cautious.

Soon, a man with workman's gloves tapped on the window.

Alexandros acted as though he didn't hear the tap. The man repeated the action, and without looking, the Rumanian finally lowered the glass.

"You the fella, this Mr. Alexandros, waiting for six crates?"

In exasperation, the small man turned to face the roughened

and bearded visage of the longshoreman. "Tell me, young man, how many shipments have you onboarded that still need to be off-loaded at two-thirty in the morning?"

"Look, mister, I have six crates left before we can get out of here. Now, either they're yours or not. And I don't know what you got in there, but if they're wild animals and the harbormaster gets wind of it, you'll have some explaining to do for not declaring it."

"Since I am the only being awake at this ungodly hour and the only one here in accompaniment of a large wagon, I suppose I am the gentleman you seek. Now that we have that established, may we proceed with the transfer of my employer's property to the wagon? He awaits the new shipment in the West, as soon as possible." Alexandros smiled. "He will need their assistance sooner rather than later."

"Goddamn foreigner." The man tossed the bill of lading in through the window and walked away.

The first of the six crates began to be lowered from the ship by block and tackle. Alexandros finally took an interest in the proceedings. He closed his eyes and opened the carriage doors. This was one aspect of his duties he never relished. The items inside the crates were famished after the long voyage from the Adriatic to France, then to the States.

He stood in the rolling fog and watched the first of the six. Alexandros did this without movement or comment over the next hour. Finally, the last crate was on its way to the wooden dock, where handlers awaited it for loading.

When they were all tied down by the Irish Teamsters hired out of Baltimore, the loadmaster walked up to Alexandros. He handed him the original bill of lading.

"There you go, German. Six crates at eight hundred and sixty-two pounds each. Sign here."

Alexandros, irritated, signed his name. "By the way, I am not German. Barbaric species." He handed the bill back to the dockmaster. "The crates are special and will assist my Rumanian master in his travel excitement. This has been planned for longer than you have been alive. Thank you for the shipment."

"And good riddance. The ship's captain says he has three deckhands missing. Says those crates upset his crew a bit. Says—"

"Sir, I do not care what any one person in your backward country has to say."

Alexandros turned to face the waiting Teamsters and stepped forward. The largest man on the front of the wagon dropped after securing the last of the ropes, and Alexandros held out an envelope.

"As promised, half your payment in advance and the full payment when you arrive. If on time, you will receive a bonus, same as last time. Inside you will find a bill of lading for the Trans-Missouri railroad as far as St. Louis. Once there, you will take on the necessary nourishment for the shipment, to be ministered through the sliding doors of the crates. Again, just as the delivery of the last shipment."

"Yes, the same as the last haul." The Teamster and his four men made sure the ropes were taut. "As far as feeding whatever you have in there, same rules apply?"

"Raw is the only requirement, and they are only to be fed in the daytime hours. The sunlight restrains them and makes you safe from"—he smiled—"a bad encounter."

"Look, I don't mind tellin' ya, Bucko, the last haul out west, I lost two of my men. Said they'll never make that run again after your last shipment, and that was for only one crate. Now we have six of 'em filled with god knows what kind of animals."

"Are you trying to say you were not properly compensated, sir?" Alexandros held the large Irishman with his cold eyes. "As I believe you and your crew will have enough to never have to work again. Are you saying that you wish me to find another man for transport?"

"Now, I didn't say that. The money isn't the problem. At night, you can hear things moving around in those crates. Gives one the willies, I tells ya. What do you have in there?"

"They will assist my employer in his endeavors out west. But if curiosity gets the better of you, sir, I'll make you a proposition. When you get the shipment to Fort Laramie in Wyoming Territory, before you leave them at the designated spot, as you did the last shipment—and if you're still curious—by all means, open the crates." Alexandros smiled and turned toward his carriage. "I'm sure that will answer all your questions quite adequately. Good evening, sir."

The four Irishmen watched the small European leave. Two men scrambled to the top of the six crates, and the two Teamsters stepped up to the seat. That was when the shuffling came from the closest of the crates. They exchanged glances, and the fog became even thicker.

The Teamster foreman looked away from his cargo. "Curiosity or not, I don't believe I'll be opening any crates when we get to Wyoming." He slapped the reins onto the six mules, and the wagon started forward toward the train station. "Not if my old dead ma's soul depended on it."

FORT LARAMIE, WYOMING TERRITORY

Father Gesepi D'Onofrio started to slowly remove the wooden splint. The leg had healed, but only after the infection had subsided and run its course. The father had been administering to the tribe in the days before winter set in, making sure the blankets and medicine from the Office of Indian Affairs were actually allotted and not just reported as such—the same corruption the War Department had seen a jump in since the war ended.

He unwound the last bandage from the broken leg and examined the area where the bone had exited the skin. The healing process had taken hold. Usually, Father D'Onofrio would not have expected a warrior such as Running Horse to submit to the white man's medicine, but in the three winters he had not seen the Sioux, the great hunter had changed. It was as if he needed to be mended and would do anything to accomplish that. His loathing and distrust of whites had suddenly vanished, replaced with a hatred of something else. The warrior had never uttered a word to the priest, but it slowly became obvious Running Horse was out to seek some form of justice for a family gone and friends left dead in the early snows of Montana.

"Well, my friend, it looks like you are free to ride and hunt once again." D'Onofrio gazed into the haunted eyes of Running Horse. The warrior said nothing while the father removed a cross from around his neck and held it out of sight. "I can see, my son, that you are saddened and vengeful. No matter what you do, the Great Father cannot restore that which you have lost."

Running Horse said nothing.

It had been three months since Running Horse had ridden into the small enclave of lodges sitting a mile out from Fort

Laramie. He had been so badly wounded; no Indian medicine had a chance at stopping the infection of his broken leg from poisoning his blood. Finally, desperate to save the unconscious man, Father D'Onofrio had been sent for by the new Catholic priest from the Vatican, Father Lexical Borras. Why the newest priest in the West had ordered him there was still a mystery. He had yet to meet the man.

Upon arriving and viewing the warrior's condition, Father D'Onofrio had thought he would be giving Running Horse his last rites. In the end, the young priest had been surprised by the resilience of the man, who steadily healed.

A scratching noise came to the flap of the lodge, and a man stepped in, covered in a buffalo robe. Father D'Onofrio greeted the newcomer with respect. With two feathers hanging from his hair, the older man appeared surprisingly youthful, but the chief was well over fifty years of age. The chief approached Running Horse and opened his robe. Several items had been brought for the great warrior: a quiver of arrows, a bow, a ball and cap pistol with belt, and a long rifle. The items were Chief Red Cloud's personal weapons. He sat down on the skins where Running Horse lay.

"You are healed, brother?"

Running Horse nodded only once, and his eyes wandered.

"I expect you will leave us. You cannot go without weapons." Red Cloud glanced away, as if not fully prepared to bring up a touchy subject. "Our people have come across signs. These are signs we have never seen before. They travel north of the Yellowstone and have covered vast distances. Whatever hunts men moves swiftly. This is all I can do for you. The old men say you have been tainted with bad medicine. That the Great Spirit has forsaken you and taken your family."

Running Horse's eyes shot to Red Cloud, but he still said nothing.

"This thing you are preparing to hunt. It does not travel alone. Strange tales come from the north. Entire camps vanish. The dead vanish. Evil has come to these lands. Even the white man has become frightened of the night. Soldiers disappear. Patrols of blue coats never return. Indian blame the white man. White man blame Indian. Yet the beast that attacked you left you alive and no other. The old men say you have been cursed for staying north when we came south to winter. They say you angered the Great Spirit."

"Old woman talk," Running Horse finally said, his eyes blank.

"Yes, but if only one believes, soon two, then three. It will spread, and you will not be welcome in any lodge or village."

"I need no one. Men I called brothers are dead. My wife, my child, torn to pieces like so much eaten grass. Defiled as no man should ever be. Yes, what I will hunt *is* evil. White holy man taught Running Horse this word—'evil.' A word which no Sioux warrior ever knew before this winter."

"This bad thing in the north, it leaves no trace other than the tracks it makes. Smaller signs of many smaller creatures follow the larger, as cubs follow the mother bear. There is disturbing talk among our people. When hunters came upon your camp last moon, they found no bodies. The blood had been buried by new snows."

"Good God." Father D'Onofrio crossed himself. "Are you saying they were consumed?"

Red Cloud ignored the priest. He held eye contact with Running Horse. Finally, he pulled out of his robe one last item. It was Running Horse's hair bone breastplate, with small bird feathers and a brass Abraham Lincoln "peace" medallion in the center—a gift from Running Horse's dead wife. The breastplate had been damaged in his battle with the beast and had helped save his life. The center row of buff bones had been slashed and broken. Red Cloud had had the breastplate restrung.

Running Horse accepted the item and stared at his dead wife's bead and bone work.

"When you leave us, brother, we will offer thoughts for you to the Great Spirit, as most say you will not return. If you do, I pray when you rejoin your brothers, you are healed." Red Cloud pulled the buffalo robe tighter around his body and stood. "Before you leave, Walking Elk wants to talk."

"Running Horse travels and hunts alone." The warrior looked up at Red Cloud, guessing correctly the intentions of the requested meeting.

"Walking Elk wants to seek the evil with you. Kicking Badger was his brother. He deserves justice as well as you."

"I hunt the beast and his followers on my own."

"My thoughts go with you." Red Cloud walked out of the lodge.

Running Horse tossed the buffalo robes aside and gingerly stood on shaky feet. Father D'Onofrio stepped up to assist, but the dark eyes warned against touching him. The priest retreated.

"Since this creature of hell knows no difference between white and red men, will you accept my church's magic for your journey?" the priest asked.

Running Horse placed the bone breastplate over his head, where it settled onto the paisley shirt someone had given him when he had been unconscious. He looked at the white holy man. The father attached the chain through the center of the breastplate and wound the cross over and through to secure it.

He held the silver cross for a moment and patted it lightly. Running Horse reached for it, as if to tear it free of the breastplate, but Father D'Onofrio put his small hand over that of the Sioux, bidding him to keep it on.

"Please, my son. I suspect you will need all the magic the Great Spirit can conjure for your journey, as he wants justice for your family as much as you...*Please?*"

Running Horse released his grip on the small cross. It dangled next to the centerpiece feathers and the ceremonial medallion of Lincoln's visage. D'Onofrio smiled.

"My new chief priest awaits me—I must go now. Go with God, my son." He left.

Running Horse gathered his belongings and the gifted weapons, then stepped out into the cold night. Most of the village had secured their lodge flaps, not out of fear of the whites, but of another threat roaming their world. They slept while the moon finally broke free of the high clouds.

Running Horse didn't pray. His thoughts were of his wife and young son, how he would track and kill the evil that took them from him.

He returned to the warm lodge, stopping when, in the great distance, a wolf's howling cry echoed through the Laramie Valley.

CHAPTER THREE

NORTHERN WYOMING TERRITORY

The small troop from Fort Phil Kearny consisted of only ten men from the Second Cavalry. Their task was to provide security for the surveying company attempting to find routes to and from the new fort just west of the Bighorn Mountains and a usable passage for customers of the new Union Pacific rail line nearing completion not far away. With much of the Plain's tribes huddling down for the winter, commanding officer Colonel Harry B. Carrington relaxed the strict security position of the Washington Indian ring when it came to the protection of contracted civilian labor.

The three large wagons of surveyors settled in for a cold wintery night, and the world of northern Wyoming Territory turned silent.

The men of the Second Cavalry huddled around their own warm fire, eating their rations of beans and fatback bacon, while the surveyors ate canned pork and peaches, considered a delicacy for the far West. The mood between civilian and soldier was hardly cordial. The greed of the East always and most notoriously infringed upon the hardships of the soldiers. US Army Second Lieutenant George Calamander was well aware of the animosity, so he attempted to keep his small troop as far away from the gentrified surveyors as he could.

"Ah, Lieutenant, but I think we should have at least four pickets out this night, sir. I don't like the way the skies are shaping up. Injuns could sneak up on us without a noise being made—one minute quiet, the next some savage boyo is lifting your hair."

The young lieutenant from Poland looked up from his spot nearest the fire and wrapped the coarse blanket tighter around himself. He was irritated by the gruff old staff sergeant, who had a bad habit of reminding him of the duty he was tasked to perform. Calamander shook his head.

"It's so damn cold out here, Sergeant, that even a stupid savage wouldn't dare to be out in it. I think the one picket will suffice." He turned back to the large fire his ten men, minus the bearded sergeant, sat around.

"You know, young Lieutenant—Indians have quite often been known to throw a surprise or two at you when you least expect it. Look at that young bucko, the one they call Crazy Horse, or the other one that goes about killing at an Irishman's pace, that Running Horse fella. I don't think they know how you boys from West Point like to play a game they've been playing for a hundred years."

"You act like an old mother hen, Sergeant."

"Yes, sir." The sergeant turned away, kicking a dozing soldier just through his anger at a young officer who thought he knew all there was to know about the West.

He placed his bedroll near his McClellan saddle, pulled out his army Colt, and slowly lay down. The sergeant huffed flakes of snow from his lips and mouth and fumed about the lieutenant not taking the necessary precautions about nighttime security. He frowned when the surveyors laughed and passed a bottle of body-warming liquor among themselves.

Another point of contention between soldier and civilian

THE CONTEST | 61

was the fact that, after seeking their protection, the surveyors ended up with all the benefits of a non-soldierly world. The sergeant placed his pistol on his chest and pulled his army blanket up to his beard.

The chief surveyor from the Continental Land Company out of Chicago, Miles Cannon, made sure his men were well provided for. It was difficult to find qualified men to brave the wilds of hostile Indian Territory for the small reward of twenty-seven dollars a month. Still, every time his fifteen men would complain, he would remind them of the poor fools in blue uniforms nearby and their meager salary of thirteen dollars a month. And while the men thought that one over, he would then supply them with the mind-numbing whiskey he kept on hand as a negotiating and rumble-quieting tool.

Meanwhile, he would collect bribes from the men running the far outposts of the nation, placing forts and settlements near their establishments by turning a route this way or that. It was very profitable for him and his company. He listened to his men laugh while his personal tent went up and the snow increased.

Cannon stared into the fire and tilted his head. The wind picked up and blew the fluff of snow around. He turned and glanced at the campfire of the soldiers, knowing the strange noise he had heard on the wind hadn't come from that direction. Cannon jumped when the voice spoke from behind him.

"Mr. Cannon, while I disagree with my overly cautious sergeant about overzealous Indians, I must tell you that your singing men and their caterwauling is quite distracting. There is far more out there in the night than mere savages."

Cannon looked up and smiled. His men started to pay attention to the officer and their boss.

"Is the young lieutenant fearful of the boogeyman?"

The young officer looked embarrassed and didn't know how to respond to the insult. He shuffled from boot to boot. The drunken civilians continued laughing at his expense. That is, until a pistol cocked.

"You heard the lieutenant. You men are making too much noise." The sergeant looked quite intimidating without his hat. The razor-cut bald head gleamed in what little moonlight filtered through the high clouds.

"You soldier boys are a little high-strung, aren't you?" Cannon said.

"If you do not silence your men, I will pull my squad away down river for the night, and then we'll see who's afraid of the boogeyman," the lieutenant replied, surprising his sergeant. He turned away from the civilians and faced the older soldier.

"Glad to see you've come to the side of the Lord, Lieutenant, when it comes to the night and hostiles." The sergeant holstered his Colt.

"Yeah, well, the sounds I've been hearing convinced me, Sergeant."

"Sounds? All I've been hearing is the voices of these fools." The sergeant was suddenly apprehensive and peered into the falling snow. "Now that they've gotten their drunk halfway home, maybe we can—"

This time, the sergeant heard it.

The sound came and went on the reinvigorating breeze. A few of the drunken surveyors stopped their snickering. Two of them even stood from their bedrolls. They had all heard the tales of the hostiles, their blowing of whistles and beating of drums, and now the stories they heard were starting to become that much more real.

"Fiddle, out here?" The sergeant slowly pulled his pistol, as did the lieutenant.

A smallish corporal approached, making the two men turn, with drawn weapons aimed. "Sir, the boys are gettin' a mite spooked."

The violin music continued. One moment there, the next the notes were snatched away by the increasing wind. When the gentle and familiar melody returned, it was again accompanied by the soft sounds of a flute.

"What the bloody hell? Some backward clergyman bring his flock out in the middle of winter?" the sergeant asked.

The rest of the surveyors had lost their taste for drink.

"Don't you think you soldier boys ought to assemble your men and investigate?" Cannon looked about nervously.

The brash young West Pointer turned angrily on the civilian. "Do not employ that word in reference to me and my men again, sir. Is that understood?" The lieutenant shifted his attention to the sergeant and the smaller corporal. "Assemble the men. Bring them to this side of the camp." He addressed a startled Mr. Cannon. "You, sir, if your men be able, get them armed, and Sergeant McCandless will place them in a defensive position."

"Me and my men are not soldiers." Cannon reached into his bedroll and retrieved a small .32-caliber single-shot pistol.

"I am most definitely aware of that, sir," Calamander said.

The wind ceased, and the music continued. This time, it was as clear as musicians playing in the New York Hippodrome.

Wide-eyed and fully awake, the men of the Second gathered. They watched the darkness to their front and the music echoing in from the thick stand of pine trees. The tune was melodious and hypnotizing, almost recognizable, but no one knew the composer.

"By God, this is strange, even for Indians." The sergeant started placing his few men in between the civilians.

Luckily, combined with the Spencer rifles of the soldiers, the civilians were outfitted with the very best. Most had Henry repeating rifles—a rifle Indians were known to kill for. The men of the Second realized that might be the reason for the nighttime activity: theft of horses and firearms.

"Sergeant, Sergeant!" came a loud whisper from one of his troopers. His Spencer was aimed at a small grove of pine trees not forty yards away.

The sergeant came forward.

"What is it, bucko?" he asked, lying down in the thick snow by the nineteen-year-old.

"Sergeant, I swear there's somethin' in those trees. Want me to shoot it?"

"Don't go a poppin' off that cannon, boy. You'll give away our position."

The soft music continued.

Suddenly, a shot rang out in the still night. A bright muzzle flash erupted from the makeshift circle of defense. A man yipped and yahooed and stood. He ran toward the line of trees. The sergeant was furious at the civilian. The music was gone, as if it had never been. The night became still, except for crunching snow.

Sergeant McCandless, the lieutenant, and Cannon followed quickly but with far more caution. The drunk surveyor who fired the shot stood unmoving when the angry officer and his sergeant came upon him. Even Cannon was angry.

"You fool, you wanna bring every damn hostile in the territory down on us!"

The lieutenant wanted an answer but stopped cold when he saw the face of the surveyor. Sergeant McCandless was the first to examine the body that had fallen from the trees. There was a violin with a clean, large bullet hole through it. The child-like hand gripping it twitched once and curled into a small fist in death.

"Good God in heaven, what is that?" the sergeant asked under his breath. He turned away from the hooded creature.

The young lieutenant swallowed his fear, and the civilian surveyor crossed himself, suddenly remembering his religious days from childhood.

"Is it a child?" Cannon asked.

The sergeant slowly removed the violin from the tight grip. He pulled the hood back from the rest of the coarse material and fell backward into the snow when the face was revealed.

"My God," the lieutenant whispered. "Tell me that isn't human."

"At first, I thought it be a child." The sergeant hurriedly gained his feet while the drunk surveyor, who had fired the shot, turned away and vomited into the snow. "But look at the skin. This abomination is older. Like an old man in a child's body."

"Dwarf," Cannon said. "I seen one at Barnum's in New York before it burned to the ground. My God, look at the teeth. Have they been filed down?"

The gruff old sergeant didn't want to know. Instead of leaning down to see, he quickly placed the muslin hood over the head of the bald and hairless corpse. Finally, the blue veins and white skin could no longer be seen as clearly. The sergeant did reach forward and close the pupilless black eyes. He kicked away the violin in anger.

The snow suddenly stopped, and the night became preternaturally silent. The shocked men backed away from the tree line until the glow of their fire warmed their cold backs.

"What was it, Sarge?" one trooper asked.

"It wasn't a snow angel, boyo. Just keep lookin' for trouble."

That was when they heard it—something like children crying. Every man, either soldier or civilian, turned and looked. It seemingly came from all directions.

"Sergeant!"

"Sir," he said, approaching the lieutenant.

The officer pointed his pistol toward the spot they had just been. "The body's gone."

McCandless looked, but all that was visible was the line of tracks and the skid mark in the snow where the small body had been dragged away. His eyes widened in fright, and the crying stopped. The snow-covered world became silent once again.

The roar shook the earth.

The snow drift protecting the horses collapsed. The canvas covering the surveyor wagons shook, like by a strong storm propelling a ship through the sea. Snowpack fell from the pine trees. The cry of an animal no man had ever heard and lived to tell about echoed through the cold night. Wide-eyed men stared into the dark.

The roar finally subsided.

"Be on the lookout, boys. We got a grizzly heading our way," Cannon said loudly.

"That ain't no damn bear, I'll tell you that, you fool." Sergeant McCandless cocked the Spencer one of his men had given him.

Then came the crash of breaking trees and thundering footsteps in the snow. How this could be possible, no one knew, but whatever had roared like a creature from hell was hurtling right at them through the tree line.

"Steady, boys. Hold your fire until you see something to shoot at."

The lieutenant and Cannon looked to the old soldier to gather their own bravery. They both went to a knee and waited, while the sergeant stood. They were far more willing to listen to the experienced sergeant now.

Again, the roar. This was not an injured animal cry. It was a sound of rage. The trees crashing to the ground were now visible. Branches and snow shot high into the air. Whatever it was came on like a train through the woods. The small body of the white-skinned and robed creature came flying, striking the fire. The men let out shocked cries. Then the roar came again. The last of the protecting trees exploded in fury.

"Fire!" the sergeant screamed when the vision from hell appeared.

The arrogance of the beast was startling. Bullet after bullet struck its neck, chest, legs, and massive arms. The creature just gathered its breath and roared again. Then, with deliberation, the monster came at the men of the Second Cavalry and the civilians they were there to protect.

The death screams of the men resounded in the night. The soft music once again started playing in the chill air, seemingly timed to the blows rained down by the great beast.

Two days later, a lone rider approached the small clearing after a night of heavy snowfall. A second horse and rider joined the first, and he watched the clearing from a small rise. Without turning to face the newcomer, Running Horse showed the boy he wasn't pleased.

"Go. I need you not, little brother."

"Three suns you say the same, yet I am here. Perhaps the great warrior isn't as convincing as he thinks?"

"Perhaps Walking Elk speaks as the fool. I travel to kill, not raid. I will not be lodging in comfort. You and men like you cannot know what lies ahead."

"Running Horse speaks the truth. But tell me, when did the great warrior achieve the gift of prophecy?"

Running Horse turned to face the young boy, who had tracked him since he left Fort Laramie. His dark eyes warned the boy he was stepping where wiser men would fear to tread.

"I am here, the same as Running Horse. I have no untruth in my words. I will not hinder the great tracker. I can help."

"Yes, I can see you can, young buck. So, if you can be of help, why is it you stand in the middle of a slaughter and not know it?"

Walking Elk looked around the rise and the clearing below. The tree line in the small distance was what he had noticed. Each had been hacked down, and their remains were lying half covered in the heavy snow, which had struck the territory for the past two days.

"I see no sign, other than the reckless regard whites have for the forest."

"And yet..." Looking at something buried in the snow, Running Horse slipped from his horse and wrapped his buffalo skin robe tight around him. His moccasin-covered foot scraped at the snow. Soon, an arm was freed, and Running Horse kicked it away. "As I said, young pup, I have no time for this. Go back to Laramie and eat warm food."

"But yet"—Walking Elk swallowed down stomach bile at the blue-clad, severed arm of a soldier—"I will follow anyway. I seek

THE CONTEST

justice for my kin also, Running Horse. The sight of slaughter does not weaken my resolve."

"We must leave this place of death. The beast and its followers have moved on."

"How does the great warrior know this?"

Running Horse climbed back onto his horse. "Their feeding is done here."

"Feeding?"

Running Horse looked closely at the nineteen-year-old boy. He smiled. "That arm is the only meat you will find from at least twenty men. The rest you will find are teeth marks on bone."

"Animals?" the young warrior asked in disgust.

"The teeth marks are from the mouths of men."

The boy's gorge rose, but he forced himself to be brave in front of the great man.

"Then it *is* men we hunt?"

Running Horse slowly started to ride off. "Go home, boy. Eat warm food and stay close to your lodge. This is a killing winter, and many bad men will come. I have seen this in my dreams. And these men will be as I—hunted. A thing I wish for."

"We seek a man?" Walking Elk asked again, catching up to Running Horse.

"No, we seek the Walker in the Night. Now, return to Fort Laramie, or you will not see the spring thaw."

"I will only follow."

"I say not another word, Walking Elk. Your destiny is now your own."

The two riders rode off further into the wilds of the frontier and never spoke of the dire warning delivered by Running Horse to a foolish young brave.

CHEYENNE, WYOMING TERRITORY

Father Gesepi D'Onofrio waited in the comfort of the station house for his guest to arrive on the stage coming in from New Mexico Territory. Outside of the Mexican population in Cheyenne, the priest wasn't usually well received at town functions or facilities. The man he was to meet was to solve the largest problem the Catholic Church faced in the frontier territories—money.

Now, Father D'Onofrio administered his flock at the Cheyenne schoolhouse. It had taken four years for the Vatican to act on his request for funding, but because of the Indian situation and the recent war in the East, most of those requests had gone unanswered. Now he would face the man with the purse strings. The man came highly recommended by the Boston Archdiocese, but Father Lexical Borras was mostly unknown to him and his small congregation.

The stage master came out of his office and checked his pocket watch. He snapped it shut, noticing Father D'Onofrio sitting on a bench. The old man made a face and returned to his small, shabby office. The Catholic priest could have sworn the gruff little man mumbled something about a "holier-than-thou mackerel snapper." The young priest was always amazed at the many inventive insults Americans in the West could come up with. He knew it was mostly a truly godless land.

At eleven thirty at night, the approaching stage noisily shot down the street, not caring any for the drunken men traversing the road. Father D'Onofrio stood, adjusted his black robe, and walked to the door, but he was shoved aside by the station master. Before the good father could say anything, the filthy man was out of the door and into the falling snow. D'Onofrio followed.

There were three passengers aboard: one woman and two men, both of which looked to be the gambling type. The woman, rouged with red and possessing a sporting woman's demeanor, huffed at the father when she entered the station house. The next man in was the hired man who rode shotgun. Father D'Onofrio watched him hurry past to warm himself by the large stove, next to the woman who was obviously there for saloon and sexual work. The two gamblers had already vanished to stake out their tables and gambling establishments.

D'Onofrio waited, but the cold and snow drove him back inside. He, too, went to the stove and held out his freezing hands. D'Onofrio slightly turned to the man with the stinky buffalo coat, who was cursing the temperature and the territory.

"Excuse me, sir?" the father asked politely.

The bearded man only slightly glanced his way, scoffed, and went back to warming himself. "Go away, Padre. Don't need no savin' today."

"I'm not here to administer to the unwashed today. I am looking for a passenger that was supposed to be on the stage. He seems to be missing."

"What do you mean *unwashed*?"

"Sir, was there another passenger on the coach?"

"No, but for the past forty miles or so, some fella dressed funny"—the man looked at the black robes of D'Onofrio—"like you, been followin' behind the stage. Kind of unnerved me and the driver. Mayhap the fella you're lookin' for."

"I don't understand. This man didn't ride with the stage?"

"Look, ask your God and leave me be. If we didn't carry him, he's not our responsibility. Now, do you mind if'in I try to get feeling back in my hands?"

"Sorry."

D'Onofrio looked out at the cold night. He turned when the lady started to leave. "Excuse me—"

The woman issued a dire warning by baring rotted teeth, opened the door, and left. D'Onofrio followed, knowing he wouldn't get any answers about his missing charge from the tired group of travelers. He slapped the sides of his robe, warming himself while he thought about his predicament.

"Apologies to have kept you waiting, Father."

A giant of a man stood under the burning and fluttering streetlamp. He was outfitted with a fur coat and had a Henry rifle. The wool cap was crusted with ice and snow, his black beard the same.

"Father Borras?" D'Onofrio asked, amazed at the size of the priest.

"That be me, my son." The man removed his stocking cap and allowed his long black hair to flow free.

"Father, I was told to expect you on the stage." D'Onofrio assisted the father with a small bag.

"The stage?" The large man laughed and looked into the confines of the station, with the warming and inviting stove. He stomped his booted feet and turned away. "Be there a hotel nearby, my son?"

"Yes, Father. Not as nice as back east, but acceptable here in Indian Territory."

Father Lexical Borras placed his rifle against the wall and took in the smaller, younger priest. "I wouldn't know about the accommodations in the East."

"But didn't you just come from Boston?"

"I've been in the territory for well over a year now, Father. I would like to know where the money allotted by our church is going to. Since I've been in the wilds, I can see any monetary concern is well justified. I will build your church, Father. Now, the hotel, please."

D'Onofrio took the small bag, deeply glad the visitor had seen the need in the frontier for church investment. Many in the territory needed saving. But learning the father had been here for the past year was disturbing in the least. D'Onofrio had only received the letter concerning the Vatican visit six months before, and said letter fully indicated the visitor had just arrived in Boston. Confused and with the sizable man following him, he decided to postpone any further discussion. This man was unlike any clergyman he had ever encountered—and that included Methodists.

"Right this way to the Metropole Hotel, Father."

"After installing me in the hotel, I have a task for you. It will take about a week, but it is something that needs to be done. I have leased a small establishment in a rather hostile environment, and I have some goods coming in by wagon. I need you to go to Fort Laramie to retrieve it and send it to my lodgings outside of a small town called Julesburg."

"Yes, Father, I know Julesburg."

"Excellent, Father D'Onofrio. I can see we will get along famously. And with that being said, I anticipate a church being built that will administer God's Word for hundreds of years to come in this land filled with heathens."

They walked on the boardwalk, past the sin of gambling establishments and saloons. Hot eyes watched Father D'Onofrio from behind, and he was tempted to turn. They were the eyes of Father Lexical Borras, and for a reason only God could know, those eyes felt disturbing.

CHAPTER FOUR

LINDELL HOTEL, ST. LOUIS, MISSOURI

Former Major Kyle Freemantle stood rigid at the front desk and stared at the clerk.

"Sir, I can only say again, we have no accommodations at this time." The small, pencil-mustachioed man looked the raggedy and road-weary traveler over, disgust etched on his face. "Perhaps the Lexington across the street may be more suited. I can send a boy over to inquire, if you would like."

Instead of saying anything, Freemantle placed his filthy hat on the check-in counter and then the Henry rifle. He scratched his beard and stared at the girlish little man.

"Major? Major Freemantle?"

The dirty man turned, taking in the blue uniform and the freshly shaven face standing behind him with a lone valise.

"It's me, Colonel Jackson. We met in New York. I see the horse I gave you at least got you this far."

Recognition finally came to the former Confederate. Without the beard, the Yankee colonel looked like most officers, which usually left a bad taste in Freemantle's mouth. But this man was of a different variety. Even before the war, he had heard of the Jackson clan in North Texas and how the disgraced older son had gone against his father, his state, and his entire family and joined the Union cause. It was then he knew the colonel to be just as much a rebel as himself, and that made the Yank at least tolerable in his thinking. He silently held out his hand. The two former enemies shook.

"You having a problem checking in?" Jackson looked from the Confederate officer he had once helped to the weaselly desk clerk.

Freemantle only shrugged, still not having said a word.

Colonel Jackson removed his own hat and placed it next to Freemantle's. "Look, if it's a matter of money, I think we can work something out here."

"Sir, no amount of money could procure something the hotel does not have. We are at full capacity. There is a special meeting that is to take place, and an entire floor has been made available to another party. I am sorry. Now, if you and your 'gentleman' friend would like—"

A red envelope slapped down on the counter. The clerk immediately lowered his eyes. He jumped back when another of the invitations came down over the first. Jackson gazed at Freemantle. For the first time in the two instances he had known the rebel major, the man smiled.

"My apologies, sir. I didn't realize—"

"No, I guess you didn't because you were too busy being an arrogant little ass. And your apology flew in the wrong direction." Jackson stepped to his left to expose Major Freemantle, who was still wearing the filthy uniform from the prison camp in New York.

The clerk bowed his head.

"Please accept my—"

"Room key?" was all Freemantle said.

The clerk retrieved two room keys from the pegboard behind him. He also rang a bell for the bellhop.

"Sirs, a clothing allowance of two hundred dollars has been allotted you for any attire that is"—he looked at the differing uniforms with near disgust written on his face—"more appropriate for the hotel."

"And who is this kind benefactor?" Jackson asked. All he knew was that the instructions in the invitation had told him to meet their contact at the Lindell Hotel in St. Louis.

"Your host, sir. As soon as you are made comfortable, we will be more than happy to awaken the store manager so you may purchase any items you may need before tomorrow's meeting." The clerk offered the two room keys. "Fifth floor. Others will join you later, I am sure."

"Others?" Freemantle asked.

"The other gentlemen that have the same invitations as yourselves." The man smiled, without the gesture reaching his beady eyes, and vanished.

Jackson picked up his envelope and handed Freemantle his. "I guess this is what they would call a 'small world,' Major."

Freemantle gestured for Jackson to go ahead. The ornate stairs were attended by bellhops, who were shooed away by the two soldiers.

"Jackson, old man, fancy seeing you here," came a voice from behind them.

Both men stopped.

George Armstrong Custer stood just outside of the dining room. He was fully uniformed, and his hair, although not as long as he was known for, was still not regulation. The sword gleamed in the light of the foyer, as if he had spent hours polishing it.

"George." Jackson nodded. "I believe I heard that you were on to your new command in Kansas."

"Indeed, I am, but it seems one has to travel there by military convoy these days because of your savage Indian friends. I leave tomorrow for Fort Riley." He stepped around Jackson and looked at Freemantle. "I seem to recognize that uniform. Who is this gentleman, Colonel?" Custer asked, not bothering to really see the former cavalry officer, other than his filthy uniform.

"Oh, you probably met more times than you would like to remember, George. Lord knows we chased him enough in the Shenandoah Valley. This is Major Freemantle."

"Seems I've heard that name mentioned once or twice while on General Sheridan's staff." Custer didn't offer his hand.

Freemantle was happy for that small mercy. He started up the stairs. Jackson picked up his own bag.

"George, good luck with the new Seventh." Jackson smiled and pivoted his back toward the former brevet general.

"I understand you have an opportunity in Wyoming and Montana," Custer said.

Jackson paused. With a deep breath, he faced the man he most despised in the world.

"I do."

"That *is* a coincidence," Custer said as a tall man walked out of the dining room. "Excuse me, Captain. I didn't mean to be so long. But I ran into an old officer friend of mine. He happens to be going northwest also." He looked away from the dark-skinned man with the white Dastar turban on his head. "Colonel Jackson, may I introduce Captain Ranjit Singh of Her Majesty's Tenth Bengal Lancers?"

Jackson held out a hand. After only a moment's hesitation, Singh took it and shook.

"As with General Custer, your reputation proceeds you, sir," Singh said with true admiration.

"Coming from a man who served in Her Majesty's Tenth, that is truly a compliment. So, it seems we've both been invited to a very special hoedown, eh, Captain?"

"So, it seems, Colonel." The bright red uniform of Her Majesty's armed forces seemed out of place after the years of warring blue and gray. The captain carried it well.

"You gentlemen have fun playing in the snow."

"George, watch your hair out there. I hear a few Indians have also heard of *your* reputation."

Lieutenant Colonel George Armstrong Custer watched the two men walk away and immediately lost his smile. He went back to the dining room and sat next to another man in civilian clothes.

"Did you get a good look at him?" he asked, picking at his plate of roast beef.

"Big man," his guest said.

"I despise that man." Custer tossed a small bag onto the table. "That's a lot of money for a man who lost his general's rank. But it's enough to make sure that our Colonel Jackson runs into mishap on his little hunt incursion. Do this and your town marshal's position in Abilene is virtually secured."

The long-haired man downed his glass of whiskey and stood.

"General."

Custer watched the man leave, knowing one of the world's greatest assassins and former spy for the Northern cause would see the job done, eliminating any future competition for any command Custer himself might want to pursue.

"Good luck, Mr. Hickock."

On the other side of the large dining room, the small man in the bowler hat watched the long-haired man rise and leave the blond cavalry officer. His practiced eye went from person to person inside the crowded room.

The man had changed his appearance the past few months, making himself less identifiable to the quarry he tracked. The beard was long, his hair dyed blond. He now sported glasses he didn't need and wore expensive clothes, which had drained his meager savings. Luckily, he had found tenants for the house he had owned with his late wife in the London suburbs, and that supplied him the much-needed funds for his travel to America.

Former Chief Inspector Robert Tensilwith, who was once hailed the best forensic detective in all of Scotland Yard, watched men and women come and go, just as he had for the past four weeks. Not one person entering or leaving the Lindell Hotel escaped his eyes falling upon them. Thus far, there had been no sign of his quarry—the mass murderer Sir Niles Van-Patteson.

"Sir, will there be anything else tonight?" asked a haughty waiter who had inquired no less than six times in the past two hours.

Tensilwith had been seated with his untouched meal in front of him. The dining room was crowded, and they wanted his table. Instead of answering the boorish little man, Tensilwith dabbed lightly at his mouth with the linen napkin and rose from the table, leaving his untouched kidney pie that the kitchen had made special for him. The waiter bowed, obviously both irritated and grateful that the man who did nothing but sit and watch other hotel guests was finally leaving.

Tensilwith walked through the lobby, his eyes still roaming, seeking out every new face. Two military men ascended the stairs. Both were too large in stature for the man he sought. A small man with a large, tasseled hat and filth-covered clothes that hadn't been changed in a month stood at the check-in counter. There seemed to be some disturbance with the desk clerk and a uniformed policeman. Tensilwith decided the heated conversation was worth eavesdropping on. After all, he figured the killer, Van-Pattenson, would have an ally or two assisting him in his flight. And on that score, no one was above the inspector's suspicion.

"Sir, I will ask once more, remove the firearms. They are not to be worn inside the city limits." The policeman with the English Bobby-style hat confronted the man with the shiny conchos riding down the hem of his black pants.

"I was led to believe that this was America's Wild West. Does not everyone have a right to defend themselves?"

"Sir, this is St. Louis, not the wilds of Montana or Texas. The most dangerous thing you can run into here is a diseased lady of the evening. Now, please remove the two pistols, or you can spend the night in my jail."

The sniveling desk clerk backed up a step when the man pulled out the twin Navy Colts and spun them. After doing so, he slapped them down on the counter in front of the startled officer.

"There, now I am as harmless as a field mouse and at the mercy of my enemies."

The policeman slid the two pistols over to the clerk. "Place these in the gentleman's luggage and inform us if he arms up again. Have a nice evening, sir." The St. Louis police officer tipped his hat and, with a suspicious look, moved off.

"Here is your invitation back and your room key. Fifth floor, end of hall," the clerk said.

The small man watched him with suspicious eyes while the clerk placed his silver-plated pistols into his valise. The clerk rang a bell, and a bellhop came forward and took the bag.

"I hope you enjoy your stay, Mr. Morales." The clerk slid an envelope toward the filthy young man, who looked at the offering with wariness. "Two hundred dollars for expenses until you strike the territories. I'll have our staff draw you a warm bath." The clerk wrinkled his nose. "May I suggest you utilize the service?"

Frank Porteguee Morales didn't respond. He kept his eyes on the uniformed bellhop taking the valise with his two weapons. Porteguee Frank snatched up the envelope. When he turned, he bumped into a nicely dressed man of equal size.

"Excuse me, sir." Tensilwith tipped his bowler to Frank. "Clumsy of me."

The bearded man moved his hat string up, securing his hat tightly, and started to move off, saying nothing.

"I couldn't help but overhear. We are to be lodged on the same floor."

"So?" Porteguee Frank said in correct English. He had practiced since reading his first Wild West dime novel.

"I guess that means, since the floor is exclusive, we must be here for the same thing." Tensilwith gave the man a false smile. "My name is Colonel Gerard Langley. *Lord* Colonel Gerard Langley, late of Her Majesty's forces in India."

Porteguee Frank looked him over from head to toe. His eyes didn't hold much respect for the well-appointed man in front of him, and the title of lord literally flew right over the South American's head.

"You're a tracker?" Frank asked with a smirk.

Tensilwith removed his hat. His grin stayed in place, his peripheral vision keeping track of the guests moving about. Porteguee Frank caught the studious way the man examined everyone.

"Of sorts, yes." Tensilwith smiled even wider and looked the tired traveler over. "By the looks of it and your marvelous-looking pistols I saw before being packed away, maybe the prey is a little different than what you specialize in, but basically the same. Big game hunting, mostly."

Porteguee Frank really didn't understand a word the man had just said. He shook his head and pushed past. While he walked, he half turned. "Whatever it is that you hunt, just remember to stay out of my way, señor."

Tensilwith watched the gaucho leave the lobby and start up the stairs to his room, hurriedly following the bellhop. He kept a smile on his face. The man he had just spoken to would bear watching. He was just the type of lowlife Sir Niles Van-Pattenson would employ. The gruff kid was either a stone-cold killer or what the Americans called a bounty hunter. Definitely a man who would find the company of a mass murderer desirable.

Tensilwith placed his hat on his head, purchased a newspaper, and sat down in the hotel lobby, like he had for the past few nights in his ever-increasing quest to spy the man who had butchered his wife.

The man stood across the street. The bandages on his face could be removed at any time, but he chose to leave them on. The man watched the well-dressed gentleman through the window of the Lindell Hotel and smiled. He had known the chief inspector would find his way to America—as a matter of fact, he had counted on it.

The detective pursuing him was good. Him finding the invitation was right in line with Van-Pattenson's plan. With the new, experimental surgery he had endured in Canada, Sir Niles Van-Pattenson had a different face, and with the help of his magnificent ear for dialects, his Western accent would be sufficient to get by even the best detective in the world.

He turned from the window, his grin growing ever larger. Sir Niles Van-Pattenson, a new man in many ways, thought his venture into the New World offered a chance for advantages beyond his wildest dreams. He tipped his hat to a passing lady of the night.

Yes, a great opportunity.

The small, fat man took the police officer by the elbow and forced him to follow. The mutton-chop side-burned man was adamant the officer do something about the situation he had yet to explain. Finally, the officer saw the problem.

"Now, as part of the greater St. Louis Anti-Chinese league, I want that man moved. What will the local populace think if we allow one of *them* to just stand in front of one of our finest hotels? What is this world coming to, I ask?"

The dark-haired man stood in front of the large window of the hotel, looking inside as if he wasn't sure where he was. After a trip of seven months, his mind was confused and his body tired.

The police officer shrugged off the hand of the city councilman and approached the stranger.

"If you be looking for Chinatown, boyo, it's about eight blocks that way. Now, be moving along."

Oishi Takanawa turned and looked at the uniformed officer. He held up his small valise and the blanket-wrapped samurai sword, then shook his head in the negative.

"What's wrong with you, heathen? I said Chinatown that way." The policeman pointed with his nightstick.

Takanawa became apprehensive until the club was lowered.

"Gentlemen, gentlemen. Please take this somewhere else. You're causing quite a spectacle for our patronage," came the weaselly voice of the desk clerk. "Look at the commotion you are causing our guests. Move this gentleman along."

The policeman, the councilman, and even Takanawa noticed quite a few of the hotel guests standing on the other side of the window, staring at them. The policeman shook his head and tried to take the newly enshrined samurai by the arm. The smaller man simply shrugged off the grip.

"Boy needs a bashing, he does," the councilman said.

"Not Chinese man. Nippon."

All three white men exchanged confused looks. Takanawa's words weren't getting through. He placed the valise down and the blanket-covered sword. Takanawa opened the valise and brought out a red envelope. The desk clerk's eyes went wide.

"Oh my God." He stepped between the officer, the councilman, and Takanawa. "It's fine, Officer. I will handle this from here. Sir, I believe you are from Osaka, Japan?"

Takanawa bowed.

"Well, isn't this something? Look, I can't take you in through the front doors. I am sure you understand. You'll have to follow me, and we'll go in the back way."

"Are you saying this isn't a Chinaman?" the officer asked while the city councilman looked on suspiciously.

"I am sure the gentleman has been traveling a very long distance. He is here at the invitation of a very well-established client of the hotel; therefore, if I would like to keep my job, he's coming inside. As much as you, I don't care for it, but there you have it. Good night, gentlemen. This way, Mr. Takanawa." The desk clerk gestured and reached to pick up the valise and sword.

That was when the samurai sword, the Dreams of Ancestors, slipped from the blanket. The sword slid to the ground, and all three men stared at the magnificent weapon.

Takanawa went to one knee and picked up the fallen blade with reverence. He closed his eyes. It was a great insult for the steel to touch the ground. Takanawa bowed his head once more and stood. The three white men watched him spin the four-foot blade six times and slam it home into the sheath with a *clack*. Again, Takanawa bowed.

"That is one hell of a knife to be toting around, boyo. Be careful with that thing."

"My God, what is this world coming to?" the councilman asked, watching Takanawa follow the desk clerk toward the alley leading to the back door.

"Ah, just be glad the Chinamen you push around don't come with toys like that. Have a good evening, Councilman."

The policeman walked away, leaving the councilman and president of the anti-Chinese league staring at the newcomer to St. Louis.

The seven invitees had arrived at the way station on their way to hell.

The man sat inside the ornate carriage, his manicured fingers resting on his cane, and watched the train from afar. The crates he had witnessed being loaded in Baltimore were once more on the move. The Teamsters placed the last of the giant crates on their wagons for movement to the paddle wheeler waiting to take them up the Mississippi and to the Missouri River. Their destination—Fort Laramie in Wyoming Territory.

All crates, that is, except for a special, small, and very intricate box no larger than a child's coffin, which the man had loaded on the carriage separate from the larger wooden crates. He smiled and patted the varnished and highly glossed wood.

The wagons with the rest of the crates rolled off. Soon, all his master's allies would be in place, and the army would be ready to do his lord's bidding when the time came. The two-thousand-year-old game was once more afoot. He tapped the floor of the carriage, and the door separating coachman from passenger slid open.

"The hotel, please."

The driver closed the opening, and the carriage moved into the cold St. Louis night.

Instead of immediately entering the Hotel Lindell, Alexandros excused his driver to go inside without him, and he remained with the carriage. He watched the outside world while the night claimed most St. Louis citizens in sleep. Alexandros had one more task to perform for his master before the festivities began in earnest after the next day's meeting of contestants.

He pulled a sizable key from his coat pocket, undid the triple lock holding the ornate box securely closed, and lifted the lid. Alexandros picked up a valise and opened it. Inside were several bloody rags his associates had recovered from an uncertified doctor in Boston. The smell of the bandages was atrocious. He slowly placed them into the box. Alexandros took out a small envelope and tossed that inside. A tiny hand pulled the long, rope-like bandage.

"Raleck, you know what to do?"

The box shook. Alexandros opened the carriage door.

"Your quarry should not be hard to find. Now go. The gentleman should be near."

A young couple was just returning from the St. Louis Opera House two blocks down the street when a carriage door opened and a short, black-clad figure flashed free of the interior. It vanished almost as if it had never been there. They watched in curiosity until the carriage door closed.

His most favored moment was when the knife first penetrated the flesh through the layers of clothing. He loved to watch the shock and the adjoining questions in the eyes of his prey when they realized their butchery had commenced. The look of anguish while his knife sliced first up and then across...The warm breath against his restraining hand and the final whoosh of air from lungs pushing out the last, precious moments of life...

The eyes relaxed in death. The power of the women's spirits exited their bodies and flowed into his own. There was a sexual rush when his third victim succumbed to his knife's embrace.

The figure in the shadows of the rancid alley slowly pulled the knife free of the young, still-warm body. The fresh snowflakes melted on the prostitute's beautiful face, and he wiped a tear away. The bandaged man lovingly moved the bloody knife to the woman's cheeks and slid the sharpened blade, as if outlining a beautiful oil painting. He was near enough to the woman's now-cloudy eyes, just one easy flick of the steel would pop free the trophy for the night.

When the blade started to pry the dead woman's eye free of the socket, a hiss and growl sounded behind the kneeling figure. The man stood and looked at the nightmare.

"Please, no sudden moves. My small associate has been cooped up for quite some time and is rather short-tempered. He gets that way on an empty stomach from long-distance travel."

The dark form's gaze went from the well-dressed man in the shadows to the hissing creature before him. Upon closer inspection, the small beast wasn't an animal at all. A little man, possibly a perfectly formed dwarf, stood menacingly. The black eyes were on the knife the bandaged man held. He lowered the blade. The hairless dwarf closed its mouth of filed-down teeth.

Alexandros stepped closer to the man and his night's work. He lifted his brows when he saw the woman's corpse. "My master had hoped you would continue to hone your skills once you reached these shores." He looked again with a smile. "This I see you have done. Excellent work, sir! Now, down to business, Sir Van-Pattenson. My associate, Mr. Raleck, has something for you."

The bald dwarf with the blackened muslin clothing stepped up to the large man hesitantly. Its dark eyes went from the man to his victim. While both Alexandros and the dark figure watched, Raleck seemed to drool at the bloody mess by the man's feet. It held out the envelope previously given to it.

"Now, now, you'll get your fill soon, old friend, as will your brothers and sisters. This lady is not your kill, but that of Sir Van-Pattenson."

Raleck hissed and, using its sharpened nails, shot up the brick wall lining the alley.

"As I said, he's somewhat short-tempered." Alexandros stepped closer to the man. "Unfortunately, sir, the corrective surgery you had in Boston will not fool the man trailing you. This makes your travel arrangements null and void, I fear. You will have to travel alone, and you will travel tonight for the area in which the contest is to be held. Chief Inspector Tensilwith, as I am sure you already know, suspects your medical correction. He will know you on sight. This is the reason for the change in itinerary.

"I most regretfully tell you, Sir Van-Pattenson, you will not be attending the meeting scheduled for tomorrow afternoon inside the Hotel Lindell. You will not be traveling upriver on the *Mississippi Queen* with the chief inspector. You will leave first thing in the morning on the riverboat *Delta Queen*. Inside the envelope, you will find a bonus of ten thousand dollars in American currency for any expenses and equipment you need to acquire for the hunt for this inconvenient change. Again, I am sorry you cannot accompany your fellow contestants to your destination. And good luck in the contest, sir. I will be pulling for you. But I must warn you, the competition is rather competent in the art of killing." He smiled a sparkling grin. "As well as yourself."

The bandaged man watched the immaculately dressed stranger walk off with a *click-click* of his cane. Somewhere above, the dwarf followed along the wall. With one last look at his night's victim, Sir Van-Pattenson turned and made for the docks along the Mississippi.

CHAPTER FIVE

The Lindell Hotel's grand ballroom was heralded as the finest west of the Alleghenies. While rivaling most Boston and New York facilities with its opulence, in reality it had never hosted anything more elegant than groups of cattle buyers and produce and fur traders from around the country. Since the monetarily draining war had ended, the ballroom had received much-needed attention and refurbishing. But it still had booked far more cattle buyer auctions than high-dollar rentals.

This day was different.

The expenses paid for the luxurious appointments and delicacies from around the world were more than anyone in the hotel kitchens and wait-staff had ever before seen. There were giant lobsters from Maine, which some of the lesser-educated far-Western kitchen staff took to be giant water bugs. There was shrimp from the Gulf Coast, blue crab from the Chesapeake, and oysters from the frigid waters off Long Island. The local icehouse had been emptied of their daily production for items like beluga caviar from Russia and steaks the size of small horses from Texas.

The doors to the ballroom were cordoned off by off-duty policemen and soldiers from the local US Cavalry garrison. These men were armed and allowed no one near the area. A large portion of the lobby had been closed off to regular hotel guests, and when they complained, their anger went without notice by management. The cost of the rental, with rooms and closures, far surpassed what the hotel made in a full year of normal operations.

The last man down the stairs that afternoon was Captain Ranjit Singh, who was resplendent in his bright red dress uniform, black pants, and white turban. He held out the red-lettered invitation when asked but was interrupted by three aggressive newspaper correspondents accosting him at the large double doors. Thus far, the reporters had attacked the invitees in packs of three and four, and the hotel had found it hard to distinguish the newspapermen from the regular hotel guests. These three would be the sixteenth, seventeenth, and eighteenth men of the press to be ejected from the premises.

"Sir, can you tell me what a captain in Her Majesty's service is doing in the United States without official orders?"

Singh looked closely at the reporter who had asked the question and was about to protest that, to the contrary, he was indeed under the orders of his government, when the hotel manager stepped in between the dark-skinned Sikh officer and his pursuers.

"This area is closed for the day, gentlemen. Our guest has an important meeting to attend and wishes no questions be asked at this time."

"Captain, there is a rumor that Queen Victoria has personally ordered you to participate in something we have not been able to verify. Can you comment?" asked another.

The Lindell's manager simply waved the police and military guard over. With a flick of his fingers, the three reporters were roughly rushed out of the lobby. The manager opened the double doors and bowed to the Bengal Lancer.

"I am terribly sorry for that, sir.".

"I would have happily answered their questions, as I have nothing to hide. I am here doing my duty."

"Excellent, sir, but I have my orders. I'm sure it will be explained inside." The manager gestured for Singh to enter.

A man of simple tastes and pleasures, Captain Singh was astounded by the spread of food. He never realized how much America had in her horn of plenty, especially after suffering such a debilitating war as the former British American colony had. The table was stacked with food, beverages, and the finest china. All was attended to by six men in hotel uniforms.

He was approached by a waiter with a tray of freshly poured champagne. Singh waved him off.

"Just water, please." He spied the other men in the room.

One wore a uniform he recognized from newspaper accounts of the war between the states. The dress blue uniform wasn't as elegant as his own, but the color and simplicity of design had just gained the respect from the rest of the world's militaries. The fledgling nation had terrified the established powers of the world with their prowess at killing in large-scale numbers. The burly man standing next to him was in need of a haircut and a shave, but he was nonetheless just as intimidating. His clothes were new, and his demeanor was one of minor curiosity. Singh suspected he was also military.

He turned when one of the servers implored a gentleman with a new suit and tie he obviously didn't know how to wear. The knot was sloppy and the ribbon of black more than just a little askew. The small man with the beard and the black hair walked away from the table with one of the large lobsters on his plate and then, when he thought no one was looking, let the lobster slip directly into a trash can, in suspicion of what it was he had just been served. He ate the roasted potatoes with his bare hands. Singh raised a brow at the uncouth gentleman.

A thin man sat in a chair, his eyes flickering from guest to guest, not even sparing the hotel staff his scrutiny. Singh's eyes fell on the most impressive man in the room, who stood aloof in the corner. The shorter man looked definitely out of place. Instead of the robes and pants the man had been wearing the night before, the Japanese invitee had on a black coat, vest, and tie with stickpin. His shoes, while looking as if they were uncomfortable, were gleaming with newness. One thing that hadn't changed was the covered blade he had resting against the wall.

The waiter returned, carrying a tall glass of water with ice in it. Singh bowed when he accepted. He eased himself toward the gentleman from Japan and slowly sat down. Singh nodded, but the man from Osaka only looked away.

The waiters left without comment.

Singh gazed more closely at the men gathered. They were all here for the same thing. As a man brought up in a constant state of war, Singh knew predators when he saw them. He looked from face to face. It was as if they all knew who each other was.

The double doors opened, and two attendants entered. They stepped aside and allowed the first, a man with a magnificent suit and spats on his shoes, to enter. The doors were closed behind the second man sporting the cane and bowler hat. He handed the latter off to one of his attendants and faced the gathered invitees. The man smiled, making his thin moustache curl at the edges. Three gold teeth stood out in the bright sunlight streaming through the ballroom windows. The man leaned back and forward on his shoes, then tapped his cane against the carpeted floor. The cane made a hollow thumping sound.

"Gentlemen, it is my sincere honor to greet you on behalf of my employer, Lord Montag Antonetnu of the Rumanian royal family. I hope that you have found the arrangements for your comfort adequate, as my master has spared no expense to see that your every need is supplied. I pray you take advantage as we—"

The loud banging of a plate sounded in the quiet room. The small man with the crooked tie was the culprit. He had stood in the middle of their welcome to make sure he was noticed.

"Can we just get down to why we are here, señor?"

"Ah, Mr. Morales, is it not?"

"Si." The man's shifty eyes went from their host to the other men in the room. He deflated some when no one made a reaction to his name being spoken. "But you can just call me what everyone else does—Porteguee Frank."

The other five men in the room had no reaction whatsoever. The man from Brazil made a sour face and sat down.

"Well, now that we have made the correction as to who you are, sir, may I introduce myself? I am Vladimir Alexandros, the representative of the man who is offering a chance of a lifetime to men who so richly deserve it. Yourselves. Now, as to your question, Mr. Morales." The small man watched the Brazilian's face once more go slack. "You have each received an invitation." One of his attendants brought him a glass of champagne, which he sipped. "That invitation was accepted, officially, as you chose to show up at the appointed time and place. The invitation is irreversible, as the game has already begun in earnest many miles from here."

"What game is that, sir?" Singh asked, trying to figure the man out.

"Ah, Captain Singh. It is truly an honor to meet you at long last. The game, sir, is *the* game. Some might call it the *only* game. The exquisite game of life and death."

"The last time in this country someone spoke in riddles like that, Americans started shooting each other by the thousands." Colonel Jackson turned to the taller man standing next to him. "No offense to this gentleman, of course."

Kyle Freemantle remained silent but did acknowledge the colonel's exclusion of him from the causes of the war.

"If you think I am speaking in riddles, gentlemen, I do apologize. Of course, this is no mere game. But it is a contest that goes back many, many years. Men who served with Constantine, Bonaparte, and Genghis Khan have participated in past contests. Along with many, many more from the world's past. The hunt you are about to embark on, if successful, will change your lives forever."

"As a recently discharged military man, what is the objective of this…this contest?" The former Confederate major snagged a glass of whiskey from the table.

"Why, to win the contest, of course."

"My esteemed colleague in the art of war has made a valid point about speaking in riddles, sir. If this continues, I will have to make my apologies and leave," Singh said.

"Again, I am sorry. My master is just so giddy with anticipation at his captured beast facing the very best hunters of men and animals in the world that I'm afraid that enthusiasm has tainted me also. The contest, as briefly explained in your invitation, is a bounty. Kill the animal as described in this"—he held up a notebook—"which each contestant will receive, and as I said, your life and the lives of people that you influence will forever change."

"All I want to know, señor, is if the offer of a million American dollars is still on the table?"

"Indeed, it is, Mr. Morales. I have the paperwork here in my bag that will show you that one million dollars in American gold double eagles has been deposited in the Bank of Boston and will be available to the winner of the contest on their request and my verification of the win."

Most of the gathered guests noticed the hint of a smile at the end of his answer.

The man from Brazil grinned, but it slowly drained from his lips when he looked at the men around him. Even if he had to murder them all, it would be Porteguee Frank to take home the prize.

"And just what animal is worth a million dollars in bounty?" the immaculately dressed colonel asked.

The small man smiled and walked over to the large buffet table. He placed the glass of champagne down and used a spoon to scoop bright red beluga caviar into a saucer. The man tasted it, made an appreciative face, and turned toward the six men.

"An animal that has cheated death since the very dawn of time. The beast can outthink you, outstalk you, and outfight you. If you think you have an advantage, he will turn that advantage around without you even knowing. He has bested the best for many, many years." The man spooned caviar onto a toast point and relished the saltiness.

"You sound as if you are describing an immortal beast," stated the bearded man in the chair, who hadn't uttered a word since his arrival in the ballroom. All he had done was study the faces of the men gathered.

"If that was what you believe from my description, I do apologize. The animal could be old, or he could very well be a descendant from a long-lived species."

"What species? Bear, cat, elephant...?" Singh asked.

The small man just smiled. He laid down the saucer and drank his champagne, then went to a wall and pulled back a curtain. Behind that curtain was a map. "Gentlemen, the parameters of the killing grounds—or hunting preserve, if you prefer."

"Indian Territory," Colonel Jackson said.

The men looked from the map to the cavalry officer, growing uncomfortable.

"Precisely, Colonel. An area of land that you have a distinct advantage in, I believe. If memory serves, my employer's research states you once served in the Second Cavalry before they trusted you enough to fight against your own family in the recent war."

Jackson grew silent. He exchanged an uneasy look with Freemantle.

"However, you are right. The territories of Montana, Wyoming, and the Dakotas will be the area in which the animal will traverse. His range is more expansive than any creature ever hunted before. As for the Indigenous population...Well, we all here are not children. Nor are we fools, are we? We know what the eventual plans and destiny for the Plains Indian will be. For men such as yourselves, you should not have a problem dealing with any threat they may pose."

He smiled, and every man in the room knew, from that moment on, they despised the small man from Rumania.

"As a matter of fact, some of them have already learned about the transplanted beast in their midst. The animal will have allies, in a sense. These allies will keep the animal contained within the specified areas depicted on the map. They will also clean up, shall we say, after the animal to keep the local constabularies and military investigations at bay. My employer is a stickler for legalities."

"Allies? I thought we hunted just one?" Singh asked.

"Oh, take no heed. You have nothing to fear from the animal's handlers. They are quite the loyal bunch when it comes to serving my master. Let's just say, they cover any...well, problems that may occur during the hunt. After all, we don't need a territorial or national government getting involved, do we?"

"These allies do what? Clean up the animal's mess?" the man with the heavy beard asked from his chair.

"Precisely, sir. Your reputation really does proceed you."

"Your invitation stated there would be seven participants."

"Keen eyes, sir. As you know, Chief Inspector, your man, Sir Van-Pattenson, is a smarter-than-average"—he looked from face to face—"criminal. It was he who had the invitation planted for your sergeant to find in his rented London flat. Very fortuitous, was it not? When my master heard of the skullduggery, he insisted on such a celebrated man such as yourself to be involved. As such, it adds a rather exciting element to the contest—men stalking men, animal stalking men, vice versa. Exciting."

"Then I will have to excuse myself. I have no interest in this... this contest." Former Chief Inspector Tensilwith stood to leave.

The two attendants locked the doors before he could open them.

"If you do that, Inspector, I'm afraid my employer will see to it that Sir Van-Pattenson is returned to England to continue his magnificent career. And I believe you still have family alive. Family I'm sure he would be very interested in getting to know."

"You bloody heathen, what kind of man are you and your warped master?" Tensilwith started toward the smaller man.

The two attendants stepped in front of him with drawn pistols.

"And for the rest of you and the thoughts that may have crossed your minds about your nonparticipation in the contest, I must warn you. My master has seen to what we refer to as a guarantor of your cooperation. Each of you are killers, proficient at what you do. You were not chosen at random, gentlemen. Many years of research has gone into your special abilities at ending life. Some claim war made you that way. We know better. Any human being that is as good at killing his fellow man as you men are enjoys such killing. Now, you will place your abilities against the greatest predator species the world has ever seen. The great beast is white in color. He will use the terrain and weather to assist in ambush. His ancient name from the time of the Caesars is 'Placeous.' Gentlemen, I wish you good fortune. And good hunting. I believe the great river and its little sister call."

Each man in the ballroom watched the Rumanian leave, and they exchanged looks. Although they despised the way in which they were described, the European was correct in his pronouncement of their character. Once someone killed the way these men had, they lost something, and that something was known as a soul. The price of their sins waited for them in the territories of the Northern Plains.

The contest was about to begin, and six hundred miles to the north, the beast described in antiquity awaited the challenge of that generation's very best. A challenge that could be the undoing of his most feared enemy, the only entity alive the royal personage from Rumania was terrified of...his own brother.

CHAPTER SIX

Cargo and passengers disembarked the *Mississippi Queen* just north of St. Louis for the less spacious and more rugged *Delta Queen*, which would take them north up the Missouri River to Fort Laramie. The passenger list had thinned out upon debarkation due to the discouraging reports from the United States Army about several tribes in the north bucking treaty authority. The reality was, since the mysterious deaths in the north started months before, the army had to blame someone, and that someone was anyone with red skin.

Large chunks of ice coursed down the river from the glaciers in the north. The *Delta Queen* easily navigated past these small obstacles keeping the few passengers on edge. Most had always heard about the instability of river craft upon the ever-changing Missouri. Each of the contestants in the "game" was assigned their own cabin, and the food supplied was not the normal fare offered to regular passengers.

Dining room number two was closed off to anyone who didn't have a red invitation, which caused some hard feelings among the men trying to gain their riches through the misfortunes of the Indian tribes in the territories—carpetbaggers, mostly. On their fifth night on the river, Colonel Jackson sat on a small crate of hardtack and dried bacon destined for the forts in the north and smoked a cigar. The first of the evening snow began to fall.

THE CONTEST

"I never liked these damn things," said a voice in the dark.

Kyle Freemantle lingered next to the pivoting steam-driven arm turning the paddlewheel.

"What's that, Major?" Jackson held out an offer of tobacco to the former Rebel.

Freemantle gestured no. "Paddle wheelers. Damn things are constantly blowing up and sinking."

"Well..." Jackson stood and tossed his cigar over the railing. "I would almost accept that fate over the one waiting for us."

"You feel it too?"

"Like we're being set up? Yes. It's like waiting for Bobby Lee to make a mistake, and when he does, you think you got him, only to find out you just stepped right into a pile of horseshit, like he intended all along."

"I never envied you Yankees dealing with that man." Freemantle sat on the crate next to Jackson. "But old U. S. Grant threw a few surprises our way also."

"I just don't like that Rumanian little bastard. He and his so-called master are lying to us."

"You sure as hell keep odd company these days, Colonel Jackson. Weren't too long ago we would be shooting the likes of your new friend there."

A tall man stepped from the shadows of the number two smokestack. He was dressed in a buffalo coat and wore a wide-brimmed white hat. Both cavalrymen couldn't tell where the coat ended and his long hair began.

"Bill, that you?"

"Well, it ain't Billy B. Jigged."

"I'll be damned. Rumor was those Missouri bushwhackers got you at war's end."

"Hell, John. If'in I have to run, no one runs faster."

The two men shook hands.

"Bill, Major Kyle Freemantle—one of those boys that would have shot you if he caught you doing your spying. Major, this is Bill Hickock."

"Mr. Hickock," Freemantle said, wary to take the Union spy's hand.

"Call me 'Wild Bill.' Most do."

"How did you sneak aboard without being seen, Bill?" Jackson asked.

"Does the word 'spy' still have meaning, you old man? Came to show you this." Hickock reached into his large coat and tossed the colonel the bag of gold given to him in St. Louis.

"This a gift?" Jackson asked without a smile.

"That is what an old friend of yours from the Shenandoah Valley thinks your death is worth. A gentleman with the most beautiful golden curls ever seen on a Union officer."

"Custer."

"As they used to say in my old Baptist church, bingo." Hickock held out his hand. "Give that back."

"May I ask your intentions?" Jackson asked.

The ex-Confederate major slowly moved his hand toward his thick coat.

"No need for that, Johnny Reb. I ain't here to shoot no one. I've come to say what I wanted to say. This man pulled my ass out of the fire more than once. One time when J.E.B. Stuart wanted it so badly, he could taste it. You boys have a good time doin' what it is you're here doing." He started to turn away but stopped, facing the two men again. "By the way, I'm not the only one George has sent north. And this one won't crawfish the golden boy like me. Tom Custer is somewhere abouts with a detachment of ten men, making sure the job gets done."

With that, Hickock tipped his large hat and vanished into the shadows, tossing his bag of gold into the air, only to catch it again.

"This just may turn out to be an eventful excursion for you, my Yankee friend."

"Your words warm my heart, my Confederate friend."

The two men, old enemies, were silent and warm, sitting by the base of the smokestack. The sound of the paddlewheel was a sleep inducer, and Jackson's eyes blurred and started to close to the gentle sound of a flute. Without either him or Freemantle knowing it, they had been joined by the nearly silent Japanese warrior. He was dressed in a more traditional robe and sandals and was without the ever-present sword.

Takanawa sat cross-legged on another crate, a blanket over his shoulders, and the flute he played looked self-carved. Jackson sat up and listened. The gentle sound ended, and Takanawa looked politely at the two men.

"Don't stop. That's one fine tune there," Freemantle said.

"It was taught to me by my mother many years ago."

"Did you leave your mother to come on this little adventure?" Jackson asked.

"She died when I was but a child." Takanawa looked at the flute and raised it to his lips. The next tune was just as melodic as the first and soothing to men who were used to loud violence and death.

While Takanawa played, the three were joined by Chief Inspector Tensilwith, no longer sporting the absconded moniker of the deceased British colonel. He puffed his pipe to life and leaned against the rail. Jackson and Freemantle watched him. In their eyes were the questions they wanted to ask about the famous murderer, the man the *London Times* coined as "the Butcher of Whitehall." Their curiosity would go unanswered. The result of the chase and murder of his wife in London was still too hard to face. He kept the killing lust for his prey private.

Suddenly, an accompanying flute sounded from somewhere above them. Tensilwith was so curious, he left his place at the rail and perused the upper rigging on the steam-powered vessel. All he saw was darkness and the falling snow.

Takanawa, although curious about the mimicry of the second flute, continued to play the mournful song about home and family lost. The other flautist was stop and go. Whoever it was seemed to be learning the tune on the fly. Once worked out, the harmony between Takanawa and their unseen guest was amazing. Finally, even Colonel Jackson stood and looked around for the accompanying player.

The snow increased, and the four men enjoyed some of the best and most beautiful music any of them had ever heard. Whoever was joining in was an accomplished musician. The melody ended, and Takanawa stood, hoping to find the person responsible for the excellent rendition of the old Japanese folk tune.

"That was mighty fine whistling," Freemantle said.

"Yes, most lovely and relaxing, I must say." Tensilwith gave up on his search of the upper rigging.

"Well, that does it for me. I think I'll get some sleep. Thanks for the tune, my friend." Jackson nodded at Takanawa. "And whoever your accompanist was." With one last look up for their mysterious visitor, Jackson left, as did Freemantle and Tensilwith.

Takanawa pulled the blanket tighter for warmth. It had taken him more than six months to learn the tune his mother had taught him as a boy, and he couldn't figure out how the mysterious visitor could have picked it up in a matter of minutes. His eyes narrowed on the false mast of the *Delta Queen*. He thought he spied movement at the top. When nothing else shifted, he bowed to whoever it was watching him and left for his own cabin.

High in the rigging, the creature known as Raleck, a human dwarf the world would come to know as a vampyr created to serve the beast, smiled. Raleck looked from the deck to the flute in his white, clawed hand. He placed the elegant instrument inside the black robe and hurried down from the rigging.

Soon, he would be soothing his master's out-of-control temper with his music—which he had done for the past seventy-five years—and he would again be with not only the beast, but his own kind. Together, they would introduce themselves and the legend of the beast to the New World.

PART TWO

"FOR EVERY EVIL IN THE WORLD, THERE IS AN OPPOSITE..."

—ABRAHAM LINCOLN

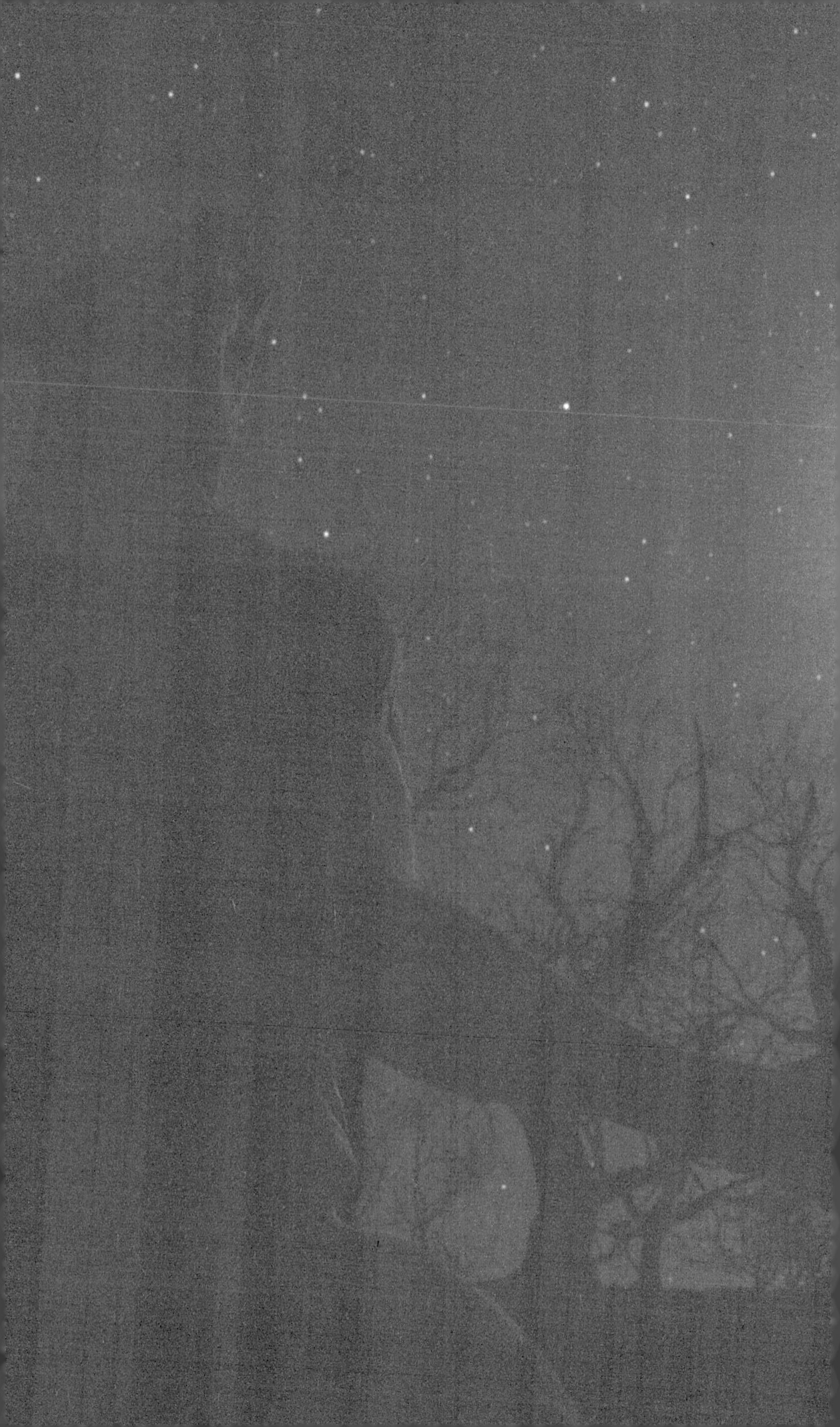

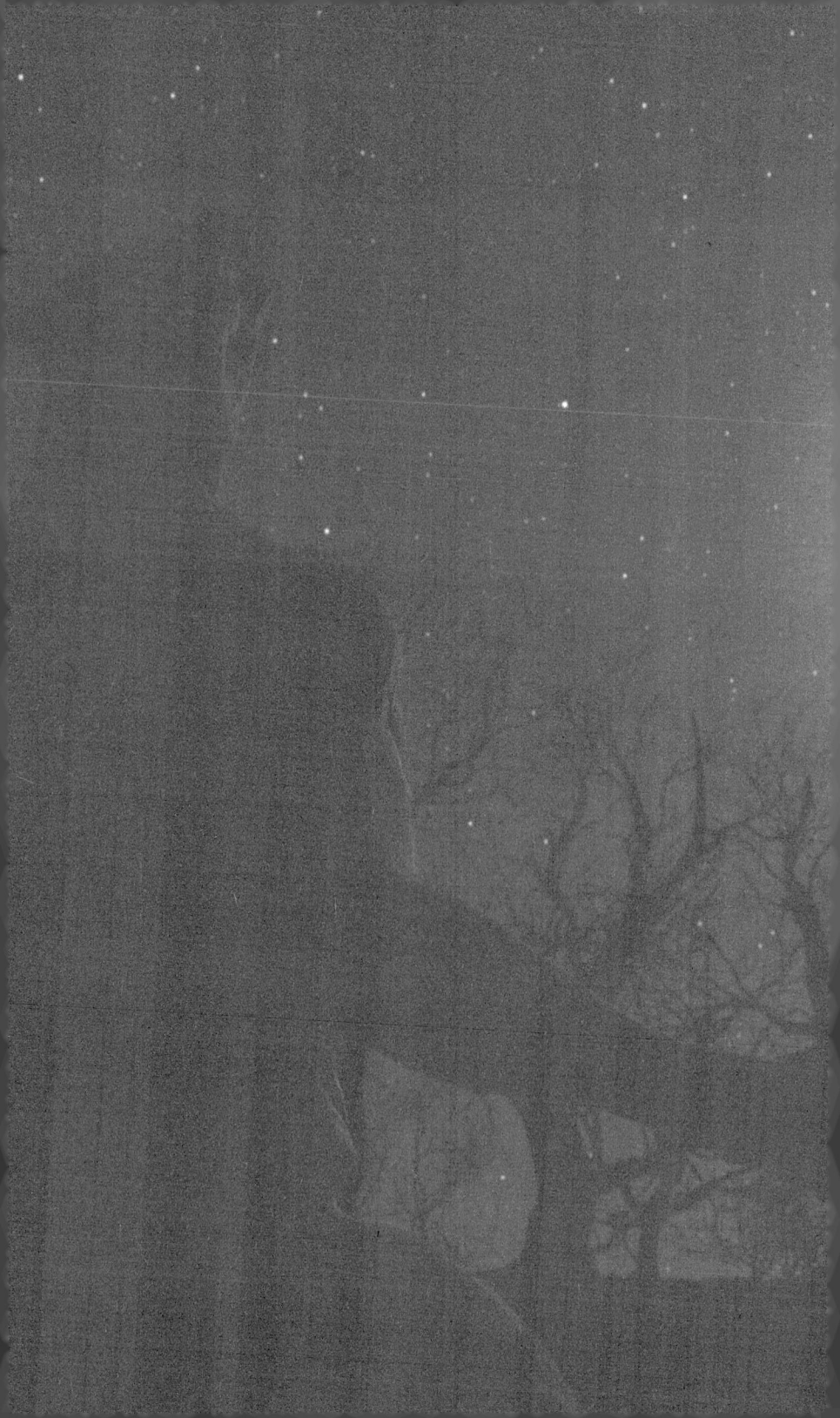

CHAPTER SEVEN

NORTHERN WYOMING TERRITORY

Walking Elk watched Running Horse kneel by the long trail of tracks. The older man was troubled. Large flakes of snow started to fill the indentations, and Running Horse quickly waved away the accumulation. After some time, he stood, pulling the buffalo robe tighter to his bruised body. He walked back through the thickening blanket of snow to his young companion and easily pulled himself up onto the horse's back.

The boy held silent his question. He had slowly learned Running Horse was not an admirer of conversation.

Running Horse scanned the horizon while the snowfall increased. He glanced back at the boy, who was waiting for him to speak. Instead, he started his horse forward. The young warrior followed, biting his tongue.

"The wendigo?" the boy finally inquired.

"This is no wendigo, boy. You must not hear everything the old ones say."

"Then what is it we hunt?"

"We have lost the sign of the beast. It has returned in the direction of the soldier fort. Now we track those that follow."

The boy was more confused than before.

"We track the small ones. It is they who track another. A beast not born of these lands, but brother-kind to the evil that took my family. This new track follows one who is brother to the wolf. But the other is enemy to all."

"We seek two?"

"You say and talk much. Learn about the world around you. White men are not the only threat to our Nation."

They rode on in silence. The young brave began to feel the world around him for the first time. A world he didn't recognize nor understand.

FORT LARAMIE, WYOMING TERRITORY

Father Borras came down the stairs of the small hotel and looked around the first floor. The dining area where several soldiers and fur traders were talking noisily among themselves smelled of bacon, biscuits, and strong coffee. Borras smiled and shook his head at the simplicity of this New World. He retrieved the long buffalo robe from his thick arm and slung it around his shoulders before stepping to the shabby front desk.

The clerk ignored the priest for the briefest moment until the large man cleared his throat. Before the clerk could ask him what he wanted, the front door opened, much to the chagrin of the café patrons and the clerk himself. A tall, skinny man braced himself against the door and forced it closed. The howling wind tore through the warm air of the hotel. The man rubbed his hands together and immediately found the large stove in the center of the small lobby. Borras ignored the man, who was covered in ice crystals and snow.

"May I help you, sir?" The clerk looked Borras up and down.

The gentleman who had identified as a priest the night before had not availed himself of the working girls upstairs nor the bath that was offered. He was still outfitted in the clothes he arrived in.

"I am looking for the young man who checked me in last night. He is to accompany me to the local freight office to recover my goods. A Father D'Onofrio."

"That young man rode a horse out of here late last night. Warned the boy about the weather moving in and the army havin' the Indians mad as hell, but skedaddle he did, like the devil was chasing him."

"Excuse me, gentlemen, but did you say 'Father D'Onofrio?'" The tall man removed his great coat, revealing a priest's worn and unwashed white collar. "I am Father D'Onofrio. Are you by any chance Father Barros?"

The large man looked the older priest up and down and knew then he had been fooled. He glared at the desk clerk angrily.

"Guess someone's not who they claim," the clerk sadly joked, quickly taking a step away when Barros gave him a withering glance.

"I must say, Father, you're not at all like you were described from my correspondence with the Vatican."

The clerk watched the newcomer slowly lower his hand in offering to the big man before him. The eyes of the grizzly Father Barros narrowed. He pulled his buffalo coat on in earnest, grabbed his Henry rifle, and took the man claiming to be Father D'Onofrio by the elbow, steering him for the door.

"A word, Brother?"

"Why, yes, of course." The thinner man grabbed his own coat hurriedly as he was rushed out into the cold daylight.

The weather was keeping everyone indoors, with the exception of a few soldiers scurrying to get themselves into the interior of nearby Fort Laramie. The large Father Barros led the man claiming to be Father D'Onofrio through the snow-covered road.

"The only thing this way is the larder depot and Teamster yard."

Barros's grip tightened on the smaller man's arm. "Yes, that is our destination, *Father*." The last word was seemingly growled down at the now-frightened priest. "I take it the young man who met me last evening was not a priest?"

"I am the only priest north of Denver. Father, you are hurting my arm."

They soon arrived through the thick snowfall. The wagon depot was empty of the weary Teamsters, who had arrived late last night and were even now ensconced in the beds of their cold wagons, out of the snow. The crates he sought were snow-covered and in the back near the rear fencing.

"The last beings on this planet I should have trusted are you collar-wearing hypocrites!"

"Father Barros, you blaspheme!"

"Call me that again and I will personally kill you. Right now, my anger is at another. There are spies here. And for all I know, you are among them. A species such as yourself will not ruin my quest to find my enemy!"

D'Onofrio was shocked when he was shoved mercilessly against one of the larger crates. He slumped and slid to the ground.

"I would inquire as to who our counterfeit priest was spying for, but your kind are bigger liars than most of the human species!" The large man kicked out with his heavy boot and caught

D'Onofrio in the nose and chin. "I have rarely been fooled in my long life, and as you can see, I do not take well to it. I am of the opinion that you are unaware of the man that boy was spying for and where he may be found?"

"Father, please—"

Barros kicked him once more, tempted to place a bullet from his Henry rifle into the cowering man. But instead, he tore off the padlock holding closed the largest crate. He hurriedly swung the door up and angrily reached down, picking the priest up by his filthy collar and even grimier great coat.

"My children may have a hard time choking you down, Priest, but their empty bellies will solve that particular distaste problem!" He threw the stunned D'Onofrio into the crate. "Breakfast is served, my children." He slammed the lid closed.

Barros left the area. The crates would be reopened that night, and then his small children would join with their brethren, stalking in earnest. They would draw his greatest enemy to the gathered huntsmen, the best killers in the world outside of himself and one other—and then the contest would truly begin.

NEAR THE HEADWATERS OF THE MISSOURI RIVER

The wagon stopped on a rise overlooking the river. The snowfall was thickening, so much so that if it hadn't been for the steady rise of smoke from the boilers and twin smokestacks of the *Delta Queen*, the large riverboat would have been impossible to see.

"There. Said we'd beat her, and we did. Now, where's my gold." The sad, weary wagon owner shook the snow from the four blankets covering the man's legs.

"It looks as if she's been here for some time," the now-unbandaged Sir Niles Van-Pattenson argued from his seat to the right of his fellow traveler.

"Listen, feller—Sir Whatever—she's just now tied up. It will be a while before she unloads. You don't know how unstable them riverboats can be on a river like the Big Mo'. This river has killed many a man. My gold?"

Van-Pattenson hated it, but he tossed the heavy buff robes off and slowly reached into the ice-covered satchel. The knife tempted to end this boorish conversation now, but he decided he was too close to his escort into the territories to take a chance of discovery. Van-Pattenson hefted the small bag of gold up and out, leaving his gleaming calling card inside. He tossed it to the wagon's driver, who eagerly opened it and lifted a twenty-dollar gold piece, biting down on it to test its authenticity.

"Well, that horse and mule will do you right, if'in you treat them right. Good luck to you, feller."

Van-Pattenson eyed the steamboat while he untied his horse and pack mule from the back of the wagon. Before mounting, he checked the supplies and made sure they were secure. He adjusted the brand-new army Colt revolver and gun belt. Van-Pattenson placed the satchel on the saddle horn of the horse and deftly slid his favorite weapon from the bag, securing it in the scabbard on his belt.

"Joe Bent's trading post is about five miles up the road there. You can usually get hot food if he's a-mind to makin' it. Coffee isn't for shit, but it's usually hot." With that, the old-timer slapped the reins onto the backs of his four mules and started to turn his rig back south. "Watch your hair, young fella."

The old man and wagon vanished into the snowstorm.

Van-Pattenson lifted the highly inadequate white hat and

caressed the hair atop his head. He made sense of the comment and quickly replaced the hat, all the while thinking there might be hostile savages observing him even then.

"Yes, watch my hair. Yes, indeed."

The two former enemies were the first to saddle and offload their horses and two pack mules from the at-rest *Delta Queen*. The other contestants were hurriedly adjusting traveling equipment. Jackson and Freemantle, cavalrymen at heart and soul, were always ready to move fast and early. Captain Singh was the third to set off. Porteguee Frank watched them leave with his dark eyes.

"I say, old man, do you plan on using anything more lethal on your journey?" asked former Scotland Yard detective Robert Tensilwith.

Oishi Takanawa cinched his harness tighter. He glanced up, first taking in the very untrustworthy Brazilian man. His eyes fell on the Englishman. Takanawa finally undid the straps around the blanket and removed the samurai sword. He half bowed, strapping it to his saddle.

"Honor demands I use the weapon of my ancestors. It would be an honor using this weapon in combat."

"Even when trying to best an animal?"

Once more, the Japanese samurai glanced at Porteguee Frank before focusing on the detective. He eased into the saddle and patted the horse, taking up the extra slack on the rope of his pack mule. Takanawa gently put leather boot to the stirrup and came up beside the Englishman.

"With a few of our fellow hunters, is it difficult to see who the real animal in these lands is?"

Tensilwith, thinking of his own quarry, could find no argument to the Japanese logic. With a look back at Porteguee Frank, the detective spurred his mount and pack mule forward.

"I bloody well see your point, sir."

CHAPTER EIGHT

PAINTED ROCK, NORTHERN WYOMING

The Mormon settlement was not more than a settler's store and a few cold and drafty cabins. One summer, it would reach the grand population of twenty-two souls. The next it would be less than fifty percent of that. Between the Indians and the hard winters, even Mormons found God's graces few and far between, and most would return to Utah Territory to be away from heathen man and an unmerciful Mother Nature.

The horse had completely given out. The young man had ridden it for two straight days, resting only an hour at a time. He had run out of oats halfway through his hurried departure from Fort Laramie. When they crested the last rise, he had finally smelled the blessed scent of someone's fire. He spurred the white-foamed horse forward, but his bootheels in the haunches of the exhausted animal was the last movement to be made that night.

The horse and its burdensome rider went down in a large snow drift. The young man once known as Father D'Onofrio was trapped by the full weight of the animal. The thought of dying so close to his destination infuriated the man. He fought hard to free the single-shot carbine from his saddle. After much struggling, it was finally accomplished. The man had lost all his strength. The task of pulling back the hammer on the Civil War relic was too much, and he dropped it. He closed his eyes, waiting for the final kiss of freezing death.

"My Lord, forgive me for my weakened body," he mumbled.

The snow started covering the man, the dead horse imprisoning him.

Suddenly, his arm was pulled hard enough for him to think it would be torn free of his body. When he passed out in pain and from the freezing cold, his body was lifted free of the icy earth beneath him.

His stiff and almost frozen figure had been positioned as close to the large hearth as they dared. The roaring fire was blazing, and the young man, who once went by the name Father D'Onofrio, sensed the heat and the blessed heaviness of the large buffalo robe placed over him. He wanted to open his eyes, but rest was what his body craved for the time being.

In his drifting mind, he realized he had something to complete. His memory fought for a foothold after the two-hundred-mile journey, which had nearly ended his life. Suddenly, he remembered and shot straight up, wracking his still-cold body with bolts of pain.

"Easy, Johnathan. You've had quite a time of it."

John Humbolt turned his head, fighting to free himself from the heavy buffalo robe. His eyes roamed the dark cabin, finally noticing the man he had nearly died to find. His reclined frame was highlighted by the flickering of the firelight.

"If you're of a mind, there's stew in the pot."

"How long, sir?" John asked, standing on weak and wobbly legs. He had no clothes on, so he scrambled for the buffalo robe.

John wrapped himself, the weight nearly forcing him to the wooden floor of the cabin.

"Just last night and most of today. Nearly sundown."

"Sir, I have news. Bad news."

"I suspected you didn't ride all the way from Fort Laramie for the northern climes winter sports." The large man in the rickety rocking chair finally stood. His darkened flannel shirt and long johns' sleeves were filthy. It looked as if he had been out for most of the day. He walked over and removed a wooden bowl from an equally warped shelf holding but a few bowls and spoons. The man eased over to the fire and plopped a generous portion of stew into the bowl before resting it in John's hand. "Sorry, it's horse. Venison and such has gotten to be quite rare up here. Bad winter. Even the Ogallala and Hunkpapa Sioux are living on agency beef. That tells ya something right there."

John Humbolt greedily shoveled the hot stew into his mouth. The heat flowing down his throat was a godsend. Horse meat or not, it was like a New York steak to his empty stomach. The man he came to warn tossed another log onto the open fire. Still, the boy ate.

"He's here." John slurped the remaining stew from the bowl.

"What's that? Couldn't hear you. It looks like you're eating the bottom of that bowl. Slow down."

John wiped his mouth on his bare skin, went to the fire, and refilled his empty bowl. "I said he's here, sir. When I seen the man you described for the past ten years, I nearly dropped a load in my pants."

"Marvelous description, Johnathan."

"Yeah, well, I thought he would see right through my little ruse as the expected priest from Cheyenne. But I guess he was just too exhausted from his ride in." John attacked his second bowl of horse stew.

"Are you sure it was him?" The large, silver-haired man stood and held his hands out toward the blazing flames.

"Looking at his eyes, I swear I could see the depths of hell in them." The younger man seemed to lose his appetite upon remembering. John had been told the stories since he was twelve years old, but never did he think he would be in the presence of *him*. He placed the still-steaming bowl down on the hearth and focused on the man, who was deep in thought. "There's something else. Somethin' I don't quite know how to make out."

The man with the silver hair but still-young face turned. "What, Johnathan?"

"Rumor, mostly. Talk around those idiot soldiers at Fort Laramie. They're spreading rumors about bounty hunters ridin' the north country."

The large man slowly shook his head.

"Mean something, sir?"

"It all fits together. The man you saw at the fort was who I feared would find me. And that rumor you heard follows his way of doing things. He has set his specially chosen hounds loose. His way of not taking chances. Brother is dusting off his old battle plans in his effort to bring this blood feud to an end."

"But these men cannot be a danger to you, sir."

"All men are dangerous, Johnathan. They have been killing on this continent since it was discovered. They are good at what they do." He faced the younger man, the orphan boy he had found in a burned-out wagon, with his family slaughtered around him. The man had raised John since coming to this country twenty years before.

"You always said that your kin are the only ones that could kill you. These are just men."

The older man smiled and shook his head. "Men have ways

beyond just killing. They can injure, wound. They can assist in the kill. Undoubtedly, my dear brother has brought those filthy ragamuffins he calls his children. Any sign of them?"

The boy looked confused. The man decided not to speak further lest he scare the boy even more than he already was. His brother would use the vampyr to herd the hunters to the hunted. They would have to make good time to the border. He suspected the bad weather would break soon, and that would help.

"The Indian we found—he received help at the fort?"

"Yes, sir. In my guise as Father D'Onofrio, I talked the fort's surgeon into helping him. When last I saw him, he was recovering, and even Chief Red Cloud was assisting. Evidently, he is a powerful warrior, well-known to his people."

"It was very clever using the priest's name. How did you come up with that?"

"I learned he was journeying to Fort Laramie from Denver. I knew the soldiers wouldn't know or care what he looked like."

"You amaze me sometimes. You think fast. Now I need you to do the same in the weeks we have ahead of us." He took the boy by the shoulders, showing his affection for the first time in years. "We'll be leaving, Johnathan. We'll ride into Canada and seek protection until winter breaks. Then we'll head to Montreal, and then I'll take you to my home in Europe. I'll have to change our names. But that's life, right?" He rubbed the hair on John's head.

"Sir, I've been with you half of my life now."

The large, silver-haired man had started gathering what they would need for their escape from a world he had thought to be safe. He picked up all three rifles: two Spencer carbines and one Henry repeater. The man stopped and finally smiled at his unofficial adopted son.

"Yes, yes, you have. And you've made my life far more than tolerable."

"Sir, what is your real name?"

The man slid his Henry rifle into a leather scabbard and faced the boy again. "You know—it's Daniel."

"Sir, if we face what you have described to me for half my life, I would like your real name. And that of your brother."

The large man eased his bulk into the old rocker, stressing its limit of endurance. He closed his eyes, weary from all the years of running. The man took a deep breath. He had not thought of his brother's name in years, hadn't even dared to think of his own. The man opened his eyes.

"My name goes back over two thousand years, when there were many of our kind in the ancient world. We lived alone and in peace with man. Until my brother, in his greed for power and jealousy of brother man, changed all of that. He hunted all of us down until I was the last. My name is *Placeous Lupa, the White*, the last true servant of God and nature, created by mysticism in the land of Carthage."

"Placeous the White," John repeated, as if the name was magical and just as mysterious.

"It has been centuries since I have heard my true name uttered by a living soul."

"And what evil is setting us on an unknown path?"

"He is the killer of man and beast and the darkest depths of the devil that warped his mind. He is *Trelzinon Khan, the Black*. And the beast is coming, and he brings his murderous horde with him...the vampyr."

THIRTY-THREE MILES SOUTH OF MONTANA TERRITORIAL BORDER

The five tents were arranged close together by the settlers. The late spring storm had set them back by two weeks and was denting their supplies before the long road across to Utah Territory and their new home, where Mormons could live in peace and security among their own kind—if they could get through the worst of the hostile Indian tribes, which remained a constant threat.

Thus far, they had been lucky. Out of the eight wagons they had started the journey with in early April, they had lost only one due to fire. The family had been saved and now continued, making it a party of sixteen with three small children.

The lone rider with two pack mules spied the camp and the lagered wagons. They weren't military in nature, so he spurred his mount forward. The snow had finally stopped just when the sun had set, and the man had brightened in mood, even when the skies became dark.

A single man stood outside the warmth of one of the large tents. He shook his head and lowered the woolen hood to the bearskin coat's shoulders. One guard, with death always near. He suspected they were fellow refugees, such as himself.

"Hello, the camp!" he called out, startling the man standing watch.

"Who you be, stranger?" The man shakily aimed an ancient ten-gauge shotgun.

"Easy, my good man, easy. I am but a fellow traveler trying to find warmth and a good night's sleep without being scalped."

"I'll ask again, stranger. Who are you?"

"Perhaps you lower that weapon before an accident occurs. The way you're shaking doesn't instill confidence in my safety."

The ten-gauge lowered slightly.

"There. Much better, sir." The man in the bearskin coat slowly eased from the saddle and tied his pack mules off on his pommel. "As I said, I am just looking for a warm place to thaw out a weary body amongst new friends."

"What is it, Joshua?" asked someone from within the tent the man was standing in front of.

"Traveler."

"Traveling alone out here? You on the run for somethin', mister?"

"Most assuredly not, sir. I am seeking warmth before continuing my travels to Oregon."

"No one travels the trail alone." The man stepped free of the tent. "Indians will lift their hair if'in they do."

"Believe me, gentlemen, in my journeys I have found far more dangerous things in the world besides the American savage. Now, is this how Americans show a stranger their hospitality?"

The two men exchanged glances. Nearby, an owl sounded out its irritation at the noise made by the intruders. Finally, the shotgun was lowered until it pointed at the snow.

"You can have my tent. You'll stay clear of our womenfolk. And you will be gone at sunrise. Understand, mister? Now, what name you go by?"

The Englishman pulled free his thick gloves. "Indeed, I will be the moral equivalent of a saint towards your women, I assure you." He held out his hand to the man with the shotgun. "My name is Niles Van-Pattenson, and you are?"

"I'm Joshua, and this here be James. The tent's right over there."

The Englishman dropped his offered hand. "Many thanks, gentlemen. May I ask if you, sir, could assist me for a moment so I can make my animals ready for the night?"

The man at the tent's flap turned back inside, ignoring the request. The one who had been standing guard leaned the shotgun against the main tent pole and shook his head.

"Let's make this fast, fella." He maneuvered around the newcomer. "I swear, you're already a passel of trouble."

Joshua turned just as the large knife sliced into his thick coat between pegged buttons. The blade was pulled up, cutting and penetrating every vital organ it touched.

"Oh, I plan to make very much trouble, my new friend." Van-Pattenson yanked the large knife free, quickly leaned over, and cleanly cut the man's throat.

The lanterns inside the tents dimmed and went out.

The Butcher of Whitehall stood and walked to the first tent. He hesitated and smiled. His body was warmer than it had been just thirty seconds before. He listened to the silence inside the first tent. The man who had introduced himself as James rustled when he lay down. Van-Pattenson ventured toward a second tent and easily and confidently stepped inside.

The killing would last for three hours. His orgasmic spree was one of his wildest dreams. America was welcoming him, and he would embrace her with much enthusiasm.

CHAPTER NINE

Colonel Jackson met up with Major Freemantle just as first light had breached the bright morning in the east and the snows had stopped. They had known they were on the same track but had kept their distance, suspecting at least three of the others were also following the same small prints, which disappeared as fast as last night's heavy snowfall could cover them. Both men stood and examined the tracks becoming more pronounced.

"I make out about thirty separate tracks," the former rebel major said. He knelt to the snow-covered ground. "Strangest tracks I've ever seen, I'll tell ya."

"Small children?" Jackson went to his horse and pulled his spyglass from the saddle bag. He walked to the top of the rise and lay down, keeping his profile as low as possible, with the sun rising at his back.

Freemantle joined him after freeing his own set of small binoculars from his saddle. He also brought over his Henry repeater.

"Six tents, no movement." The colonel adjusted the single-lens glass. "Seems late in the morning for settlers not to be getting ready to move. No sign and no smoke from a breakfast fire. I count trails in the snow where at least twelve horses or mules hightailed it out of here. This isn't good, my rebel friend."

"Smell that?" Major Freemantle lowered his binoculars.

The morning breeze brought the smell of death. Both men

had come to know it so well after the war back in the East. The coppery smell of blood.

"Seems we have a visitor." Jackson adjusted his view.

The slim, small form of the Japanese samurai shed his blankets and robes, down to his silken clothing, and cautiously eased into the silent and deserted camp.

"It's our Japanese buddy, Takanawa," Freemantle said. "Damn, that's one big knife the boy carries."

The samurai sword gleamed in the bright sunlight when the warrior eased it through the flap. Takanawa did not continue inside. He slowly backed out, moving his head from side to side, scanning the area for any immediate danger.

"Let's get down there and see what's spooked our Oriental friend," Freemantle said.

Both old soldiers rose as one.

Takanawa stepped away from the first tent and approached the second. He eased back the flap, sword at the ready. It was the same inside. He was beginning to wonder what sort of country he had arrived in. Takanawa had heard stories of the barbarity of Americans but had found the tales hard to believe. Women, children butchered. There have been similar instances in his own country, but the deaths of the young and womenfolk were, in most circumstances, collateral damage and never intentional.

"Easy, old man." A pistol pressed into his spine. The man's approach had not been obvious until the last second.

If he needed, Takanawa would be ready.

"Easy, I don't wish to shoot."

"Nor do I wish to strike you, Detective Tensilwith." Takanawa eased the razor-sharp end of his ancient blade away by centimeters.

The man from Scotland Yard knew he had been matched in deadliness and stealth.

Tensilwith eased the hammer of his Webley pistol down and lowered the gun. "Touché, old man, touché."

"I do not understand your words." The samurai put his weapon at his side.

"It means you had a Mexican standoff and would have killed each other for nothing. We've been watching. You both arrived at close to the same time," said another voice behind them.

The major and the colonel aimed their Navy Colts in the direction of the Japanese man and the Englishman. They had gotten the drop on the detective and samurai. Both men stepped past and looked inside the tent. The Englishman joined them.

"God in heaven," Freemantle hissed under his breath. He had seen much death in the past four years, but never anything as brutal as this.

Three women, two children, and two men had been scattered among blankets and clothing. They were nearly not recognizable as human. The blond hair was the giveaway for the children.

"It is the same in the other tent, and I suspect in the other three." Takanawa, seemingly having had enough, walked into the center of the small camp. His sword was still at his side, for his own comfort.

"The small tracks?" Freemantle asked.

"I don't see any of those around. This is something else."

"If you speak of the same child-like footprints I have been following most of the night, they seem to have led off to the west, away from here. The thing that did this has a distinct calling card." The detective leaned down and rolled what looked to be one of the women over.

He ripped open her shabby dress, and both old soldiers recoiled at the cold way the Englishman treated the dead.

"You will see, gentlemen, the hearts are all missing." He nodded toward the other corpses inside the tents. "Or the hearts, I should say, have all been removed. I'm afraid there is not just one beast hunting us here in your country, but two. And by the looks of those small, strange tracks, maybe a hundred more. The culprit here and the criminal I seek is the man who slaughtered my own wife, all because I got close to catching him."

Both the major and the colonel exchanged looks. They followed the detective and were soon joined by a suspicious Takanawa.

"Mr. Tensilwith perhaps now would be a good time to tell us your sad story, and don't bother to leave out the small details," Jackson said.

The four men gathered to hear the man from Scotland Yard's tale of woe.

A quarter of a mile away, the hatless man adjusted the scope on his long-range Sharps fifty-caliber rifle. He had brought it along with this forthcoming intention in mind. After all, the fewer bounty hunters there were, the greater the chance the reward would be his. His aim fell on the larger of the two soldiers, who was standing the closest to his second intended target—the rebel major. He figured the Scotland Yard detective and the fool with the sword could wait. They could not be as formidable as the two experienced killers trained by war. Porteguee Frank started placing pressure on the rifle's hair trigger.

The sound of the pistol being cocked at the back of his head froze the finger before the trigger could be pulled.

"That wouldn't be exactly cricket, now would it, Mr. Morales?"

The Sharps fifty caliber lowered slightly from the Brazilian's deadly aim. Porteguee Frank eased his head around and recognized the man immediately. Captain Ranjit Singh. His white turban was the only item of clothing the Brazilian bounty hunter could make out. The rest of the Sikh's clothing was of the purest white. Even the bearskin coat had been bleached in St. Louis before departure. The man had just been labeled by Morales as a serious threat.

"I have no binoculars. The scope was the only way to observe from this distance."

"Perhaps pulling the hammer back on your weaponry is the best way to adjust for distance?" Singh gestured with his Webley pistol for Morales to release his weapon. "I think it best you remove your rather formidable pistols and belt also."

Porteguee Frank reached under his own heavy coat and undid the belt's buckle. His mind flashed. Perhaps he could outdraw the aimed Webley.

Singh slightly tilted his head, as if saying, *Are you sure?* Morales removed the belt, the shining Navy Colts gleaming in the morning light, and laid them on the snow. He angrily stared at Captain Singh.

"So, you are to leave me to our intended quarry, unarmed, señor?"

"Perhaps I will leave it to the men you were about to murder in cold blood, Mr. Morales."

"Then who would be the murderer, Captain? You or me? You know the gringos will kill me and barely slow their hunt."

Singh un-cocked the British-made Webley pistol. He quickly glanced around him and, with his knee-high right boot, kicked at the Brazilian's twin Colts in their gun belt, sending the weapons toward the murderous Porteguee Frank.

"Perhaps I will not get that chance, my South American friend. We are being watched with ill intent. Up in the trees."

Frank warily glanced at the high pines around them. He saw nothing, but he pulled first one pistol, then the other, letting the belt fall to the ground. "Which tree?" Frank slightly raised the Colt in his right hand.

"As far as I can tell, all of them. Perhaps maybe a hundred sets of eyes." Singh holstered his Webley inside his white fur coat. "May I suggest we act as though we have not observed them and perhaps move on to where we have more guns?"

"If I go down there, they'll kill me. You know that. I'll be better off up here. Better odds, señor."

"Your actions thus far will be between you and I. But if you so much as look as devious as you had earlier, I will tell the Americans of your earlier intent. Even then, I suspect you may have better odds at staying alive down there than facing that which observes us here." Singh eased back to his horse and pack mule and pulled himself into the saddle. "Stay or go." He started down the small rise. "That is up to your good judgment."

It wasn't long until the sounds of Porteguee Frank climbing onto own horse and mule quickly followed Captain Singh through the thick snowpack. The Sikh smiled.

TEN MILES TO THE SOUTHEAST

Walking Elk lay beside Running Horse. As hard as he tried, he could not make out the identities of the small line of men and horses trudging through the snow in single file. He could only distinguish the lead figure. The man traveled ahead of the ten others. The figures were dark in shape against the white snow. If they were soldiers, he did not know what trail they followed.

"Soldiers?" Walking Elk asked quietly.

Running Horse shimmied back on his belly until he could stand unobserved. The young warrior mimicked his actions.

"You are learning to hold your questioning until you have at least half the answer."

Walking Elk had just been slightly insulted, but he held his tongue, knowing the rebuke could have been much harsher from the man who was not used to teaching young fools.

"Yes, soldiers. They follow two differing trails: that of the small ones who foul the night air, and white men. The small ones who follow lead the soldiers to what they really hunt."

"Soldiers hunt other white men?"

"Yes, the small ones of the night, who leave a trail that the soldiers have followed."

Running Horse pulled tighter the buffalo robe and then mounted his horse, careful to avoid knocking the haunch of bear meat. He had scavenged it the night before at the site of a strange kill, by an animal he also tracked. Running Horse had four trails to travel and hoped they all converged at some point. The small night men, the soldiers, and the white men they followed...but his eyes narrowed when he thought about the true quarry: the beast who had destroyed his life.

Running Horse turned and looked at the younger warrior. "This battle will start soon. Many will die."

"I do not fear what lies ahead of us," Walking Elk said with false bravado.

Running Horse started his mount forward once more to follow the soldiers.

"And this is what makes you a fool, young one. Showing and feeling fear does not make a warrior a coward."

SIXTY MILES SOUTH OF THE CONTESTANTS

The tent was larger than most cabins on the frontier. The servants hired on the East Coast had started their long ride back to Fort Laramie, where they would return to Boston and many other East Coast cities. Their employment on the Plains had come to an end after setting up the elaborate camp.

Not one of them questioned the strange man's resistance to having any security measures in hostile Indian Territory. His death wish was none of their affair, just as long as they had been paid in advance for the facilities they had set up for their very eccentric European employer. The master's private chef, steward, and the rest of the hired men would keep their silence as to who had employed them.

Vladimir Alexandros poured himself a glass of cognac and placed a log inside the woodburning stove. The departed servants had struggled it off one of the eight wagons used to build the palace of a camp. After all, his master might have been used to the wilds of nature, but Alexandros certainly was not. He sipped the warmth of the liquor. The manservant, resplendent in his frock coat and tie, snapped open the pocket watch and read the time. He relaxed.

Alexandros was early for his rendezvous with his lord. He walked over and eased himself into the large leather chair ensconced close to the stove—also something the servants had wrestled with for the fifteen-hundred-mile journey from Boston. Alexandros listened to the preternatural silence of the heavily forested area he had chosen to meet his lord and master in.

"Raleck, strike a tune, will you?"

From outside came the sounds of crunching snow and a bow sliding across the taut strings of a violin. A sweet chord was struck gently, producing one of the most heartfelt melodies familiar among the servant's memory—a favorite of both master and slave.

"Excellent choice, my small friend."

The large tent flap separated, and the frame of the murderous dwarf entered. His bow fluidly skated across the antique violin, a gift to him from his master. The small creature, known only to a few as the mythical vampyr, swayed while he played.

The myth of the vampyr had been perpetuated by the master of their ancient house to keep the unwashed from his doors. Since the myth was nothing but that, just a story the beast had to create, what human could he use other than that of the unwanted? The disfigured? The dwarf? He created a human who hated the clean and the righteous more than the discarded.

Raleck was the oldest of the vampyr, the master's favorite, the leader of over a hundred of his fellow outcasts. Brought up in pain and torture, love, and hatred of man, they had been raised with the taste for the rawness of human and animal flesh. Not even Alexandros, their keeper, dared to step in between the wishes of his master and the murderous moods of the vampyr. While he listened to the excellent playing of Raleck, Alexandros waved his free hand through the air.

Suddenly, the music went silent.

He opened his eyes, hearing what Raleck had sensed a split second before. Alexandros turned his attention toward the small vampyr. The old dwarf relaxed, so he followed suit. Their master was close by.

Alexandros emptied his crystal glass at the sound of hooves plopping through the now-slushy snow. It had been three years since he had been in his master's presence, and the man always filled him with feelings of dread and abject amazement. A true wonder of an ancient and forbidden world. A magic whose secrets had been lost to the sands of time. Alexandros stood, refilled his glass, and swiftly swallowed the burning liquid, falsely fortifying his courage. He placed it and the decanter down on the small cloth-covered table. Alexandros glanced back at his chef and the server, nodding to indicate their duties could commence at any time.

Raleck was the first to react when the single horse and rider slowed and stopped just outside the large and well-appointed tent. Alexandros straightened, making sure his frock coat was sharp. He closed his eyes in anticipation of the most powerful being on the planet. A small commotion preceded the ugly hiss of joy from the small vampyr.

"And it's very good to see you also, my old friend. It has been much too long." The deep voice switched from roguish English to the more comforting language of their homeland. "Suntem gata să ne începem munca?"

Alexandros understood the question. It was formed in the more modern Rumanian language—which he suspected was for his personal benefit—instead of the ancient language of the Wallachian or Transylvania Boyar's from the time of Vlad Tepes, otherwise known as the *Impaler*. That dialect had been a dead language for over fourteen hundred years. At any rate, Alexandros swallowed hard while the master asked his murderous vampyr if he was ready to commence their work. The disgusting creature, who had once been a dwarf human, snarled and snapped with anticipatory pleasure.

"This is good, old friend." The words entered with the man known as Trelzinon Khan, the Black. He allowed the vampyr to snake down his chest, where he had been embracing him.

Raleck hissed when Alexandros took a step forward and bowed.

"Alexandros, I see you have made it to the New World with your needed accouterments?" The Khan removed his gloves and bearskin coat, looking around the avarice-filled accommodations.

"I am not the type to go as native as yourself, my lord. I could never blend in like you. As the Americans say, I would stick out like a sore limb." Alexandros straightened, embarrassed by his over-exuberance for creature comforts.

"That would be, *stick out like a sore thumb*, I believe the saying goes. Whiskey," the Khan ordered, glancing at the servant awaiting his orders. He roughly tossed his heavy coat and gloves into the pristine clothing of Alexandros.

The man knew he had displeased his master in some manner, but for the life of him, he couldn't think of where that failure could have possibly been. For the years they had been separated, every order and request had been fulfilled to the letter. After delivering the American-made frontier whiskey to the giant of a man, the servant was hit roughly with the large coat thrown by Alexandros. The Khan downed the fire-branded whiskey without so much as a hiss. He held out the large glass for it to be refilled.

"My painstakingly planned trap is thus far not going the way I anticipated it to go."

"My lord, all of your chess pieces are in place, according to your instructions."

"You failed to report to me that my brother has a young ally. This boy was lying in wait for me at Fort Laramie while disguised as, of all things, a priest." The master angrily downed the second tumbler of whiskey and tossed the glass to a stupefied Alexandros, who fumbled and dropped it to the tarp-covered floor and hurriedly retrieved it. "Now dear Brother is warned that I have finally found him after two hundred years of searching. He may be a weaker foe, Alexandros, but he is still a killer, like his older brother. Knowledge is power, and now that power has shifted because your spies failed to report this alliance. He obviously knows now that he needs alliances to survive what I have planned for him."

"Surely, with the entire vampyr army here, this can still be accomplished."

The Khan glared at Alexandros. "If that were your only failure. Now we have soldiers chasing my hunting party. For what reason, I cannot fathom. Can you explain why this is happening?"

Alexandros lowered his head. He had done nothing in error, but he could not protest his innocence at this particular time. Alexandros started to force his apology from his trembling lips, but Raleck hissed, stepping forward with a threat. Perhaps now was not a good time for further conversation.

"Raleck, leave him be...for the moment." The Khan knelt so he could look at the tiny vampyr in his black eyes.

The bald-headed creature with lily-white skin half bowed. Even it was afraid to behold the master for too long.

"As I said, we have work to do. Whatever this group of soldiers are planning for my contestants, they must fail. I do not want them to interfere, as the hunters will soon pick up the trail of the hunted." The Khan placed his giant hand on the top of the vampyr's head. "Your horde has done well herding the contestants toward my quarry. Very well indeed. Now, take fifty vampyr and assist my hunters if these soldiers have ill intent on their minds. Go now, my friend, taking caution to go unobserved. My special invitee, the Indian warrior, already has spied my minions, so steer wide of him until the right time."

Raleck bowed all the way through the thick tent flap and was gone.

The Khan finally walked toward the long cloth-covered table, with the silver service and chafing dishes. The large man took a whole roasted chicken and bit the bounty in half. He was famished after his long ride. The master swallowed, took up the large decanter of whiskey, and gulped deep. He tossed the remains of the chicken onto the pristine cloth.

"Now, do you wonder that my anger at you had not brought about your immediate demise, Alexandros?"

The servant remained silent. Anything said in the negative could quickly bring on that end. He barely nodded.

"Because of one major success you have made in contribution to this venture of killing my brother: the procurement of our exceptional Sir Niles Van-Pattenson. What a wonderful addition to this exclusive club we have. Your recommendation through letter to me here in America had brought us an element that may just surprise my brother and possibly other factors that may fail me in the near future."

Alexandros half bowed his head at the praise. But was it praise, or was it a threat? It would seem if he failed the master again, he just might have supplied the Khan with his own replacement.

A replacement more to the liking of Trelzinon's darker side.

TWENTY MILES TO THE NORTH

The two men stood just inside the tree line, looking slightly downhill at the tents with binoculars. The six figures in the camp moved bodies from three of the tents into a fourth. The man with two crossed swords on his cap lowered his field glasses and glanced at the soldier to his right. This man had been specially chosen by him after receiving orders from his older brother while en route to Fort Riley in Kansas Territory.

Tom Custer smiled.

"This shouldn't take long. This task seems to fit your calling to a 'T,' Corporal. Even if you and the men are observed, it looks like these marauders attacked and murdered a camp of settlers. The killings would be justified in any court. Besides, you'll have the protection of my brother to back your case."

"I'll have the protection. What about you, Captain?"

"This isn't the job for a captain in the United States Army, Corporal. You and your men were chosen specially for your past handiwork."

"You mean, chosen 'specially' because we were the only eleven in the guard house."

"Accurately spoken, as always, Corporal. Now, when you're done, your records will be expunged and your discharges waiting for you."

Tom Custer looked at the waiting ten men behind them. They were anxious to get this job done.

"Well, it's a long ride to Fort Laramie and then an even longer ride to Fort Riley. You boys, when done, head straight for the winter camp. I'll see you there in no more than eight weeks."

The bearded corporal shook his head. "Typical officer," he mumbled.

The rest of his murderous detail surrounded him.

Tom Custer quickly spurred his black roan forward. "These woods are startin' to give me the willies."

"Come on, all the hostiles are down south, wintering it out near Fort Laramie."

"'T'ain't the Injuns I'm worried about. It's those damn small tracks we keep comin' across. Now, who's the target down there?"

"Cap'n said go ahead and kill all six. No need to pick and choose. But I did notice two that had the bearing of officers. Just the way they walk and such. So be mindful. The rest look as worthless as teats on a bull."

The eleven men removed their single-shot Springfield carbines from their McClellan saddles and took cover behind the line of pine trees.

"And you two just came across each other in the wilderness?" Colonel Jackson asked.

"Yes. Mr. Morales here was relaxing under these wonderful

pines," answered Captain Singh. "I hope we're not intruding, gentlemen."

"Is that what you were doing, Morales, relaxing and taking in the afternoon sun?" Freemantle eyed the young assassin.

"I was just watching and wondering which of you may have killed these poor, innocent pilgrims, señor."

The eyes of Freemantle, Jackson, Singh, Takanawa, and Tensilwith remained on Morales and didn't waver. They all noticed it was Singh who had Morales's scoped rifle. Each also watched closely the right hand of the Brazilian, in case he made a play for his silver-plated Colt revolvers in their ornate holsters.

"Boy, a warning: If you try and crawfish on us, you'll never leave here alive." Colonel Jackson pulled out a telegram he had received en route from St. Louis. He handed it to Detective Tensilwith. "I was informed of your past exploits, Señor Morales. It seems your choice of bounties includes womenfolk and children."

All eyes chanced a look at Porteguee Frank once more. They were all killers of men, but each had killed for either self-preservation or duty.

"I am guilty of all you say, señor, but only those that steal from others. I am paid legally to do so. I believe each of you in your own way are paid to do the same. Am I mistaken?"

They had no argument to Porteguee Frank's declaration of guilt. In turn, they focused on the snowpack at their feet.

"Ah, to hell with it. I'll just say I don't like this little son of a bitch. There, now make a move that makes me nervous, boy." Freemantle's fingers touched the Colt at his side.

"Easy, Major. We may need this little bastard before this madness is concluded." Jackson hefted one of the pilgrims' discarded lanterns and struck a match. He placed the wick on high and tossed it into the tent, where they had arranged the bodies of the immigrant families.

The tent and its cargo of dead innocents exploded in a false warmth, belying the cold winter around them.

"Gentlemen, since I have no desires toward your quest for monetary gain, I will simply say good luck. I have another godless quarry to pursue. A quarry whose victims you are now burning, through no fault other than their desire to help a fellow traveler." Tensilwith removed his bowler hat in respect to the burning family before them. "From here, I have to do my duty, not only for my wife, but to remind me I am a human man."

"Inspector, I will only say good luck. I'm sure each of us will agree, your mission here is far more important than ours, as you chase the real beast out here." Jackson removed his gauntlets and extended his hand.

Takanawa watched the English detective ride away to the east. The man had a monumental task ahead of him. The animal he sought was cunning and merciless. Beside Takanawa, the others watched the two tents burn with the murdered travelers inside. They gathered around the wagons.

"This is where I leave you, men. I've always done better on my own. I figure if I could reconnoiter the Shenandoah Valley ahead of Phil Sheridan, I can stay ahead of whatever's out there. 'Sides, this Johnny Reb gives me hay fever."

Freemantle gave the Union colonel a crooked grin and was about to wish him luck, when a shot rang out and echoed inside the valley. The first bullet struck the seat of a wagon, tearing a large chunk of wood free. Pieces ricocheted and hit the Brazilian, who yelped and immediately dove for cover. The others quickly followed suit. Snow was soon being churned up all around the wagon. The five men tried to pinpoint where the ambush was originating from.

"Gentlemen, since I am the only one without long-range weaponry, may I suggest I use speed to take cover in that wagon over there? This should give you an adequate view of our hidden foe." Takanawa slowly slid the samurai sword free of its sheath.

"Damn, Japanese fella speaks better English than I do." Freemantle drew his Navy Colt revolver, wishing he had his Henry closer by than with his horse and saddle fifty feet away.

"Speaking English wasn't exactly a Southerner's strong suit, Freemantle," said a smiling Jackson. "Mister Takanawa, I think you're a damn fool, but I don't have a better plan in mind. Pretty soon, whoever's up there is bound to get lucky and hit something."

"Do not take too long to react, gentlemen." Takanawa shimmied back and then stood and ran.

The other four men watched the bullets chase the samurai. Puffs of snow churned up, and ice crystals filled the air. Takanawa dove for the cover of the second wagon, and more bullets tore into the wooden seat.

"I have them, señors. I suspect maybe eight to ten. Madre Di Mios, these men are not amateurs."

"By the sound of those reports, they're using Springfield single-shot carbines. Too short a range for that distance. I believe the prophecy of your spy friend, 'Wild' Bill, is more accurate than I would have given him credit for. I suspect Yankee soldiers in that tree line up there, and being Yank marksmen is the reason why they haven't chewed us up yet. May I suggest—"

Before Freemantle could finish his sentence, the young Porteguee Frank slid out from under the cover of the wagon's bed. Even Singh wasn't quick enough to stop him. They watched a demonstration of firepower and deadlier marksmanship than any of the four men had ever witnessed.

With heavy caliber bullets zinging all around him, Porteguee Frank pulled both sparkling silver Colts from their ornate holsters and opened fire into the tree line. He emptied the twelve shots and, before the others could blink, was swiftly reloading.

To cover him, Jackson, Singh, and Freemantle started emptying their own revolvers. There were yelps as several of Porteguee Frank's earlier shots found something other than air or tree. One thing the men would never do again was doubt the killing prowess of the kid from Brazil.

The cavalry corporal looked around him. Two of his men were dead, and another two were shot up good. Whoever was down there would chew them up if they stayed.

The two men with the command look of army officers emptied their pistols. These men were not even close to being as accurate at the kid with the wide-brimmed black hat and the fancy shooting rig. The smaller man had reloaded and then started firing again. Two bullets ricocheted off the tree the corporal was taking cover behind. He shook his head in anger.

"The hell with Tom Custer and his idiot brother. It's time to go!"

The corporal waved his remaining men to get to their horses. He left the two dead men behind. At least one of the wounded wouldn't make it far. Half of his left eye socket had been shot away.

"We ridin' to Fort Riley to join the rest of the Seventh?" a private asked.

Each fought to get cold boots in stirrups.

"Don't think the general and Tom Custer would be too welcoming when those men down there find our dead companions, do you? No, we'll head to Fort Kearny and then maybe back East, where no one will find us."

The remains of the ambush started retreating hard and fast, the way Tom Custer had ridden earlier. The mission was down to nine men, with two wounded badly. They would be lucky to make it through Indian Country.

But the soldiers were about to discover hostile Indians were the last of their problems. The vampyr had caught up to them and awaited their arrival in a place of their choosing.

The horde of fifty vampyr ate well that night before returning to rejoin their master.

CHAPTER TEN

SIXTY MILES SOUTH OF THE CONTESTANTS

Trelzinon Khan stood just outside of the huge tent, forsaking the heavy coat and comfort and warmth of the soft accouterments preferred by his manservant, Alexandros. He took in the first real sunshine of the winter months. If truth be known, the large man, this immortal, preferred the wintery days. They reminded him of his chosen adoptive home, Rumania.

The Khan raised his face toward the late afternoon sun. The orange orb started to settle toward the peaks of the Rocky Mountains. He sniffed the air, and a smile came to his stern visage. Much blood had been spilled that day. But maybe four or five of his small vampyrs would not be returning home to their master. That meant Raleck and the others would be in mourning for those lost.

"Alexandros," he called, without losing sight of the setting sun.

Ensconced in his heavy frock coat, Alexandros hurriedly stepped from the tent. He held a crystal glass of cognac in his right hand and bowed to the back of the large man.

"My lord?" he answered.

"Tonight, my vampyr will mourn the few that they have lost in battle with the soldiers. But I do not want them to be alone.

I shall join them. Have those fool servants in there gather much wood and place the makings of a large fire in that clearing over there, where the trees block out the wind."

Though his chef and servant would not enjoy the order of manual labor, Alexandros still didn't hesitate to answer his master. "Yes, my lord."

"With the exception of the barest minimum rations for you and the servants to live on, I want your larder of uncooked meat emptied out and your stock of wine available for my vampyr tonight." Trelzinon Khan faced Alexandros for the first time since calling him from the warmth of the tent. "And Alexandros?"

"My lord?" he answered, shocked he would have to give up most of his delicacies and his precious wine stores to that ravenous horde of miniature freaks.

"My advice to you is not to leave the confines of your palatial tent tonight. You'll not only have festive and very angry vampyr out and about, but it has been months since I have made the change. And remember, my children and I have been known to be quite out of control at this time of the month. After all, the moon is full, and I will be at my strongest."

The blood rushed from Alexandros's face. This time he didn't hesitate. He swallowed the burning cognac before he acknowledged his master's orders.

Trelzinon Khan smiled and laughed. The last of the sun vanished behind the mountains.

"Hurry, my brother, Placeous, hurry. My wishes are nearly fulfilled."

SIXTY MILES NORTH

Running Horse was the first to smell the rank odor of coppery blood. It sat on the steady breeze, like a buffalo robe would cover the floor of his lodge.

"What is it?" Walking Elk asked quietly.

"Learn to use your other senses rather than your mouth, young one. Now, what is different since the sun left the sky?"

Walking Elk gazed up at the stars, which sat as if on a black blanket.

His young companion was confused, so Running Horse dismounted. "We have stepped into a killing field, young one. Many deaths have met with the small tracks."

Walking Elk swallowed, finally realizing what he had been smelling all along but didn't recognize what it was: blood. He slid from his horse's back. Both men slowly started forward.

Running Horse eased a round into his Henry rifle without making the typical metal on metal lever noise. Walking Elk removed his small factory-made hatchet and pulled out his old Colt's Dragoon pistol. They paced through the softening snow for twenty yards before Running Horse stopped, cold from the sight meeting his eyes.

"The Great Spirit has left this place," Running Horse mumbled under his breath.

His gorge rose, and Walking Elk leaned over, trying desperately to breathe his sickness away.

In the tall pines surrounding them hung the carcasses of at least eight men. Hard to say the true number because some had been strung up by their boots, with the top halves of their bodies missing. Others were headless, with their torsos absent. It was a slaughterhouse. Blood had congealed at the base of every hanging corpse, and a murder of crows cawed loudly at the intrusion by the two Sioux Indians.

"The same soldiers whose trail we picked up." Running Horse noted the hundreds of tiny prints left by the attackers of the soldiers. They were leading back the way they had come. With one last glance at the murderous scene, Running Horse took Walking Elk by the arm and turned him away.

"Do we leave them?"

Running Horse angrily stopped and pulled the young warrior close to him.

"We leave them as they are. These soldiers went looking for trouble, and they found it. And young one, if you had opened your eyes instead of your mouth, you would have seen that parts of these soldiers were eaten. We camp for the night. This night will not be fit for men." He glared at Walking Elk. "Or for young fools that call themselves 'warrior.'"

Around them, even the crows had left the free meals hanging in the trees. Tonight, an ancient evil would reveal itself once more.

The lone rider ventured slowly into the kill zone not long after the departure of Running Horse and Walking Elk. The man guided his horse and pack mule directly beneath the hanging bodies of the soldiers of the newly formed Seventh Cavalry—unofficially the regiment's first casualties on the Plains.

The man lowered the scarf and breathed in the recognizable perfume of his own kills. He reveled in such splendid killing. Whoever had done this was surely a rival to his way of doing things. Either they would be a challenge or an ally who might be willing to share such exquisite knowledge.

"Wonderful work. I must find who is responsible for such glorious carnage." He spurred his mount forward.

Sir Niles Van-Pattenson could easily follow the plethora of small tracks leading off to the south.

The evil of the world was starting to seek each other out in the new winter of 1867.

Raleck was the first vampyr to arrive back at camp. The others would wait for him to seek them out. The murderous creature scratched at the main flap of the tent.

"You have returned, I see. Your speed amazes even me, old friend."

Raleck was startled by the stealthy approach of the master. He quickly turned and hissed in fright.

"Come, was your mission successful? Are my human stalkers safe from the soldiers?"

Raleck rasped out his answer in barely understandable English. "Yessss, Massster."

"Good, good. How many did we lose?"

Raleck lowered his head in shame. He slowly held up four fingers and a thumb. The nails were long, sharp, cracked, and dirty, marred with fresh blood.

"A steep price for the failures and ineptitude of others." Trelzinon Khan's black eyes darted toward the tent and his servants inside. "Did you observe anything else, old friend?"

Raleck nearly fell when he bowed, stumbling in his long, black robes. Trelzinon swiftly moved to the shaking vampyr, thinking his oldest might have been hurt. When he forced Raleck to look up, something else was on the creature's face. The vampyr had been frightened of something he had seen on the trails.

"You're shaking, my friend. The mighty vampyr fears nothing. What has you upset?"

It took a moment, but the old dwarf made eye contact. The fear in his eyes was replaced by apprehension. His master despised departures from his planned maneuvers. Raleck started to speak in broken English, but Trelzinon placed a large hand on his bald head. The Khan could not understand the vampyr's words.

"Easy, old friend. Use the old tongue. And be precise."

"*Fratele Placeous, nu este aproape de vânători. El încearcă să scape în nordul îndepărtat.*"

Trelzinon Khan appeared as if he wanted to strike out at the small creature. The beast's anger rose like a volcano. The large man collected himself. If he struck out, he would be doing so foolishly, for no reason other than his coward brother avoiding fighting once again.

"So, brother Placeous is not close to the hunters as we planned. He tries to escape to the far north. Canada, I suspect. He plans on running to Europe." Trelzinon plucked the vampyr from the ground and allowed the claws of the creature to crawl to his mammoth shoulders. "Tell me, old one. Can you catch up to him?"

"Yessss," Raleck hissed, beginning to relax.

"Alexandros, I know you are listening. Come, join us."

An embarrassed Alexandros stepped from the warm tent. The last rays of the sun vanished in the orange sky.

"My lord?"

"Tomorrow, I have a special mission for you and Raleck."

The vampyr hissed and spit at Alexandros.

"It seems dearest Brother has decided escape and evasion the better alternative to valor. He has avoided my contestants by at least four miles. Raleck says he and his boy companion have camped for the night. I know this to be true, as I have guessed at his intent."

Alexandros's stomach wanted to free itself of its inebriating contents. "What does my lord wish of me?"

"I suspect I know the reason Placeous flees. The boy may actually mean something to him. And since I owe this child a stern piece of my mind for his little deception back at Fort Laramie, I wish you and Raleck to bring the boy not to me, but to my contestants. This may draw Placeous out to the hunters."

"What if my lord's brother catches us?"

Trelzinon lost the smile he had been wearing since coming up with his makeshift plan. He glared down at his manservant.

"Then he catches you, fool. Then your duties will be fulfilled, and you would be free of service to your master." He started to turn but stopped. "Both of you will leave after my greetings to my children. I suggest you get some sleep. My old friend here will awaken you long before sunrise."

The frightened man vanished back into the tent. Trelzinon reached back and pulled free the strong grip of the vampyr. He held him out by the hood of his robes, allowing him to dangle a moment before setting him down.

"You have done an outstanding job today, old friend. Now is the time of your reward, and your brothers and sisters shall join us. Gather them all in the clearing over there. I will join you at moonrise."

There would be celebration on this moon-filled night. Raleck smiled, showing his filed-down teeth, and jumped high in his joy.

"Go, gather the horde. I want good music, and you will have delicacies and wine all of the New World will be envious of. After the celebration, we shall speak of the 'morrow."

His minion ran off to gather his siblings. Even the Khan's children were expendable for what was to come. He would spare nothing to stop the only being on earth who could possibly stop *him*—his own little brother, Placeous.

Captain Singh watched the distant fire from a half mile away. Just before sundown, the figure of Major Freemantle had built the camp and readied for sleep. Even from that distance, the former Confederate officer seemed as weary of this night as Singh. It was something on the air. Singh couldn't quite put his finger on it, but tonight was very different from the other nights he had spent in the strangest of lands.

"You feel it also, Singh-san," came a voice from the darkness.

"Takanawa-san."

"You go with a cold camp this night?" Takanawa moved into the light of the rising moon, his horse and pack mount in hand.

"There is something out there tonight, and I have sensed its presence. I suspect you feel the same?"

Takanawa removed his saddle and tossed it to the snow-covered ground. He only nodded at the East Indian. Takanawa removed a small satchel from the pack mule, relieving the animal of its burden. He tossed the leather bag to Singh, then hobbled the mule and his horse to the other two. All four animals were getting skittish of something they smelled upon the night air.

Singh removed a thick piece of buffalo jerky from the pouch and chewed the cured meat while Takanawa tended to his animals.

"As I do not trust the Brazilian boy," Takanawa said, "I believe we should stand watch on differing shifts."

"My thoughts also," Singh replied. "The little killer is very good at firearms, but who is to say what he aims them at? I am thinking it's of little consequence to him."

"You sleep first. I will wake you in three hours." Takanawa glanced to the sky and the blossoming full moon.

"Would you like a firearm, my friend?" Singh nodded toward the sheathed samurai sword.

"No. I do not plan to be in camp. I will watch from the rise. This is so we are not surprised in the night by man or beast. In any case, my friend, may I suggest you have your weapons unholstered until sunrise?"

"I have no other plans than that."

Two lines of clouds crossed the bright orb of the moon, and the night became preternaturally still. It was as though the world around them was absorbed in cotton.

FIFTEEN MILES TO THE SOUTH

Raleck sat upon the bounty of raw meat and cases of wine. The huge fire roared at the center of the clearing, and a sweet violin played in the near distance. That was soon joined by a flute and then a piccolo. Another violin chimed in, then the soft tap of a tambourine. The vampyrs had been taught by a blind gypsy woman from the Carpathian Mountains inside Rumania. Being impaired as she was, it had been impossible for the old woman to see the inhuman students she tutored.

From the tree line surrounding the clearing, the glowing eyes of Raleck's brethren watched the bounty of food, ravenous hunger aching in their small bellies. Suddenly, a roar sounded through the night air. It reverberated powerfully from tree to tree, hill to hill, and valley to valley. Trelzinon Khan had transformed. Snow fell from branches, and rocks slid down hills.

The echo of the roar slowly faded. The clearing was silent, and Raleck hopped free of the bounty of meat and wine in anticipation of his master's appearance.

They sensed the beast's approach long before it appeared through the large pines. Many of the vampyrs cried out in fear. The crunch of snow was heavy, and a second roar filled the night's sky. Raleck fell to his knees and buried his bald head in the cold snow. Then he heard it.

The black beast stepped free of the tree line and reared its giant muzzle to the moon with another roar. This time, animals that had remained through the winter storms and prophecies of the coming evils panicked and, from thirty miles around, fled their cover. The eight-foot-tall werewolf shook its massive head and long ears until the last roar was pushed from deep in its bellowing chest. It raised its muscled arms toward the full moon and screamed the wail of centuries past.

The floodgates opened.

Led by Raleck, the remaining hundred vampyrs broke from the shadows. The beast turned in a circle, but it wasn't defensive. The small creatures surrounded it, like the followers of the Christ would have hailed Him. They fought each other just to touch the greatest animal on Earth—a beast created through ancient necromancy by a civilization trying desperately to fend off the advances of a young Roman Empire.

The vampyrs reached, cried, and fell to the ground at the great beast's clawed feet. They worshiped the creature they had been created for.

The werewolf leaped twenty feet off the ground and suddenly was gone. There were cries of anguish and fear that their master had left them. But it was Raleck who screeched and pointed at the bounty of food stuff offered by their great benefactor. The vampyrs attacked the meat and wine—a rich bounty they had never witnessed in their entire tortured lives.

From thirty miles around, the men of the contest sat up in their bedrolls upon the sound of the devil's roar. The contest was about to begin in earnest. No one would sleep well that night.

CHAPTER ELEVEN

VALLEY OF GHOSTS
NORTHERN WYOMING

Johnathan awoke two hours before dawn. It had been close to four hours since his adoptive father vanished into the night, just when the full moon had risen in the sky. The predawn was as silent as he had ever heard before, and he brought his bearskin robes up to cover his lower face. There had been not only the howls in the distance, but also the much closer refrains of the nearby wolf. He hoped Placeous was nearing the end of his night terrors so he could return to camp. There was something out there in the night, other than the ancient magic of the two brothers. He sensed the sinister presence of something unknown to him.

The large fire he had built dwindled to coals. Johnathan had eased his arm out of the bedroll and reached for another log to bring his warming blaze back to life when a small, black-booted foot slammed harshly upon his extended limb. He tried desperately to pull his arm free, but a tremendous power held it in place.

Raleck smiled down at him with a murderous longing. It raised one of its arms high in the sky to strike the frightened boy, who had once called himself Father D'Onofrio.

"Don't, you fool. The master said the boy is to be unspoiled."

Raleck hissed, and for a moment, Alexandros thought either the vampyr was going to go through with the killing blow against the boy or turn on him instead. Alexandros ignored the threat, resplendent in his finest wool coat, went to his knees, and quickly gagged the boy's mouth before he could scream a warning to his companion, who was close by since the moon had set. He roughly turned the boy over, pushing Raleck away, and expertly tied his hands behind his back. Alexandros was good at the work he used to do on his way to gaining his status in Rumania. He had been responsible for many kidnappings through the years at the master's pleasure.

Raleck still hissed. After the celebration the night before, his bloodlust was up, and it needed to be satiated.

"Drag the boy to the horses." Alexandros climbed to his feet. He gazed around the darkness with great apprehension. "We must leave, as brother Placeous may return at any moment. Leave five vampyr here to cover our escape to the south. Have them kill the horses and pack animals. That should slow him down in his pursuit."

Deep in his throat, Raleck growled, not liking the man giving him orders. But in his warped and damaged mind, Raleck realized he had to obey on behalf of his master. The vampyr turned and made his way to the hobbled horses and mules nearby. He would take out his anger and frustration on the innocent. He was soon joined by ten other vampyr.

Placeous's strength weakened when the moon vanished from the sky. It wasn't that he lost his power for the change; it was that his strength was at its zenith with the full moon. And until the partial moon rose tonight, he would still be the strongest beast in the world, except for his brother, who was very practiced in his ability to draw power through his hatred of the world around him.

The distant sun crept closer to breaking into the sky in the east. The giant white beast suddenly stopped. His muzzle flared, and his keen sense of smell caught the odor of blood. He momentarily went to all fours, still as tall as a small mustang of the Plains. He wasn't alone in the early morning. The danger had to be dealt with before the rise of the sun, or he could very well be left to the mercy of whatever was waiting for him.

The beast rose to his massive two-legged stance and started forward. Somewhere deep inside his animal mind, he feared for his adopted son. Through the fog, Placeous the White moved forth to confront the waiting evil.

The five vampyr were anxious to prove themselves after last night's celebration. They were still inebriated from food and drink and thought they could at least hurt the master's brother, whom each had heard tales of but had never seen in the flesh. The smell of blood from the slaughter of the horses and pack mules made the small creatures nearly uncontrollable. Each drew a blade from their robes and waited for their prey.

Suddenly, the first line of trees seemed to explode inward toward the now-cold camp.

The White roared when it spied the first vampyr, which leaped in midair, curved blade poised to strike. The beast's thick, six-inch clawed hand shot skyward and caught the struggling vampyr by the bald head, claws sinking deep through its skull. It squeezed, crushing the head to pulp. When its senses caught the smell of another leaping from a nearby tree, Placeous slammed this second one down with the headless body of the first. The beast tossed the body of the first once more, catching a third scurrying down from the middle of another pine. The small vampyr screamed in agony when the blow broke its brittle bones.

The first soft light of dawn hit, and Placeous howled once more. The animal's strength waned, and he went to his knees. White fur began to drop free of his morphing skin. The crush of excess bone in his muzzle cracked and broke free, his bone structure returning to that of a human. The leg bones shortened, and the muscle tone immediately shrank to its original form. Placeous dropped to his stomach until his body's resurgence to his human self was finished.

That was when the last two vampyrs attacked.

One jumped on his naked back, stabbing three times. The second attempted, with all its strength, to raise the chin of Placeous so it could get a clean cut across his throat. Placeous bucked, sending the vampyr into the hot coals of the waning campfire. Its black robes immediately blazed into fiery life, and the creature ran screaming in agony. Placeous took the final assailant by the throat and squeezed with one hand until bone and cartilage gave away. He tossed the foul-smelling vampyr into the reignited fire, where it burned brightly.

Placeous entered the tent, instantly collapsing into the empty bedding where his adopted son had been. He buried his face into the buffalo robes, gripping the fur and sinking to his lowest depth of despair. His brother had caught him unawares and knew how to strike him where it would hurt the most. The idea he had thought so clever, of sending the boy to spy at Fort Laramie, had come back to haunt him. He had possibly condemned the innocent to a brutal death. His white hair tangled and matted; his head shot up. He would not condemn his son to the destiny Trelzinon had planned for him.

Placeous exited the tent and stood naked in the bright morning light. His face became a mask of pure hatred and vengeance. His days of running from his older brother were over. He would face that which he had spent nearly twenty-seven hundred years hiding from.

He would have to kill Trelzinon Khan.

Raleck was not happy being relegated to the treetops. The master's distrust of the usually competent Alexandros was equaled only by Raleck's hatred of the human manservant.

Raleck hissed and spit in anger while he retreated to the camouflage of the high pine trees, and Alexandros slapped the struggling bundle on the pack mule.

The boy was not cooperating in being still and silent. Alexandros reached out and removed the brand-new Henry repeating rifle from its leather scabbard. He walked a few feet away from his horse and the hostage-laden mule and loaded the first round of .44-caliber ammunition. It would take at least ten to get the attention of the contestants nearby.

With one hand, Alexandros pointed the store-bought weapon to the sky and started firing. He ejected shell casing after shell casing until ten shots had been exhausted. The last echoed across the Valley of Ghosts until it finally faded. He lowered the weapon but kept it at the ready. Alexandros walked to the nearby campfire and held out his free hand for warmth.

From a nearby hilltop, Running Horse and Walking Elk watched the heavyset man two miles away. The strangeness of his actions had confused the two Sioux Indians until the first two riders approached from the north. The two men, both covered in heavy hunting wear, made Running Horse aware something deeper was at play here in the Valley of Ghosts.

Soon, a lone rider approached. And another. Finally, one who came on with speed rode over the far rise. There were now more white men in the valley than wildlife. Five men had answered a signal from a sixth.

Running Horse and Walking Elk had also spied the small creature stalking off toward the tree line. This was one of the foul ones whose tracks they had followed for the past week.

"Come, we will observe to find out what these men want in the Valley of Ghosts." Running Horse eased back and walked to his horse.

Walking Elk silently did the same.

All five men thought someone was in a firefight, that they might have come across a hostile band of Indians. It was an unwritten law of the Plains that assistance had to be rendered when hostiles were concerned. The last to arrive was Colonel Jackson. He had been three miles away, and both rider and horse were tired from their sprint into the valley.

Jackson looked from one man to the other, keeping his rifle at the ready. That was when he noticed the well-appointed man they had met in St. Louis and the Henry rifle at his side. Jackson nodded at the other contestants, knowing they might not have been destined to seek out this bounty without the aid of each other.

Porteguee Frank kept his black-gloved hand on one of his silver-plated Colt revolvers. The boy seemed unhappy to be among the others once more.

"I thought we were to see you in Boston, Mr. Alexandros?" Jackson threw his own rifle over his shoulder and reached out his gloved hand for the warming fire.

"Circumstances have changed, Colonel Jackson." Alexandros shifted his attention from Jackson to the Sikh Captain, then to a suspicious Takanawa and to Freemantle, finally eyeing an anxious-looking Porteguee Frank, who appeared to be in a killing mood. "I see we are missing Detective Tensilwith. I pray he has not met an untimely end?"

"He has other business to attend to. Now, may I ask why you may have alerted every hostile within twenty miles of our location?" Jackson finally felt warm and revived enough to express his anger adequately.

"My question exactly, old boy," Captain Singh agreed.

Alexandros smiled at the five men. "You see, gentlemen, your prey was trying to go to ground. He and his companion were making a run for the Canadian border, to escape to Montreal and then back to European soil."

Porteguee Frank started to make for his horse, fearful he would be cheated out of his just reward.

"Easy, Mr. Morales. I am sure his plans have been altered in the past few hours," Alexandros stated, stopping Morales from his flight.

"So, now we hunt a man and a companion also? Do we hunt a beast, or are we bounty hunters for your employer?" Freemantle asked. "Because I don't do that kind of work."

The others were now looking at Alexandros with utter contempt. Even Porteguee Frank despised being lied to.

"Gentlemen, the beast is, and can be, a man, though I suspect you will run into the darker of the two strains very soon." Alexandros glared at the five contestants, not bothering to hide his disdain for their ilk. He moved to his pack mule and slapped the still bundle hard, bringing a small yelp of pain from within.

Alexandros untied the bundle from the mule's back and roughly threw his cargo onto the thick snow. There was a loud grunt, and the occupant started cursing like a Pennsylvania coal miner. Alexandros used a large knife and cut the leather straps, freeing the boy's covered head.

"You son of a bitch!" the boy screamed. "This chance you're taking will not work. My father is no fool. He won't risk his life for an adopted orphan. Don't you think he's faced tougher choices in all of his life? Give me a chance, and I'll kill you myself!"

"What is this?" Takanawa asked.

"Yes, what have you done? Kidnapped a child?" Captain Singh grew angry at the mysterious way the hunt had gone.

"This is a guarantee. Assurance that the beast you hunt comes to you. May I suggest you be alert, gentlemen? I am afraid my employer has—how do you Americans say—'poked the bear.'"

"I am just about sick and tired of your riddles and outright lies, you European ass." Freemantle reached for his holstered Colt.

Jackson caught his hand and held it until the Confederate major relaxed. Alexandros strode to his horse.

"Free the boy, keep him as bait, kill him...Regardless, gentlemen, your scent will be on him. The beast *will* find you." He laughed and hefted his heavy frame onto the saddle. "In any case, friends, I'll see the survivor in Boston, where the reward awaits."

"What if *you* don't make it out alive?" Jackson asked loudly.

"Arrangements have been made for our banker to see to it that your just reward is forwarded to you. Good luck, gentlemen."

Jackson looked at the retreating form of the Rumanian, then down at the angry boy still tied in his blankets. With a smile on his face, he glanced from one contestant to the other. They realized exactly, just as Jackson did, what needed doing.

"Mister Morales, since it seems we no longer need Mr. Alexandros as we thought, will you explain to him our disappointment in his behavior?"

It only took a moment for the Brazilian to grasp the point of Jackson's question.

"Si, señor." He pulled the right Navy Colt from its concho-covered holster and used his left hand to fan the hammer. Six balls flew from the Colt as rapidly as any of them had ever seen, once again impressing everyone.

The six shots caught Alexandros in a six-inch-diameter circle in the center of his back, sending the manservant flying forward over his horse's head. His blank eyes stared up at the cloudless early-afternoon sky.

A mile away, Raleck, who had been perched on a limb like a black vulture awaiting a meal, witnessed the murder of Alexandros. Instead of fright, he smiled and jumped up and down so hard, the accumulated snow fell from the tree. The human he despised most in life for his closeness to his master was finally gone. And died in a most violent way, which the diminutive vampyr admired very much. Killed by a boy with as much talent as Raleck himself.

When his exuberance had ebbed, the vampyr jumped from the tree at tremendous height and started running to his master with the devastating news of Alexandros.

Running Horse allowed his eyes to narrow when he finally came close to what he had been tracking for the past two weeks. His quarry and the little creatures were inexorably linked to one another. How, the great warrior knew not, but his instincts told him they were linked together as father and son. The small creatures would lead Running Horse straight to the beast that had murdered his family and those who had depended upon him to see them through the winter months.

"We are close now, young warrior. The time is coming when you will drop foolish things and face the world of mystics. Come, we follow."

His final retribution and revenge were now at hand.

PART THREE
THE PRIZE AWAITS

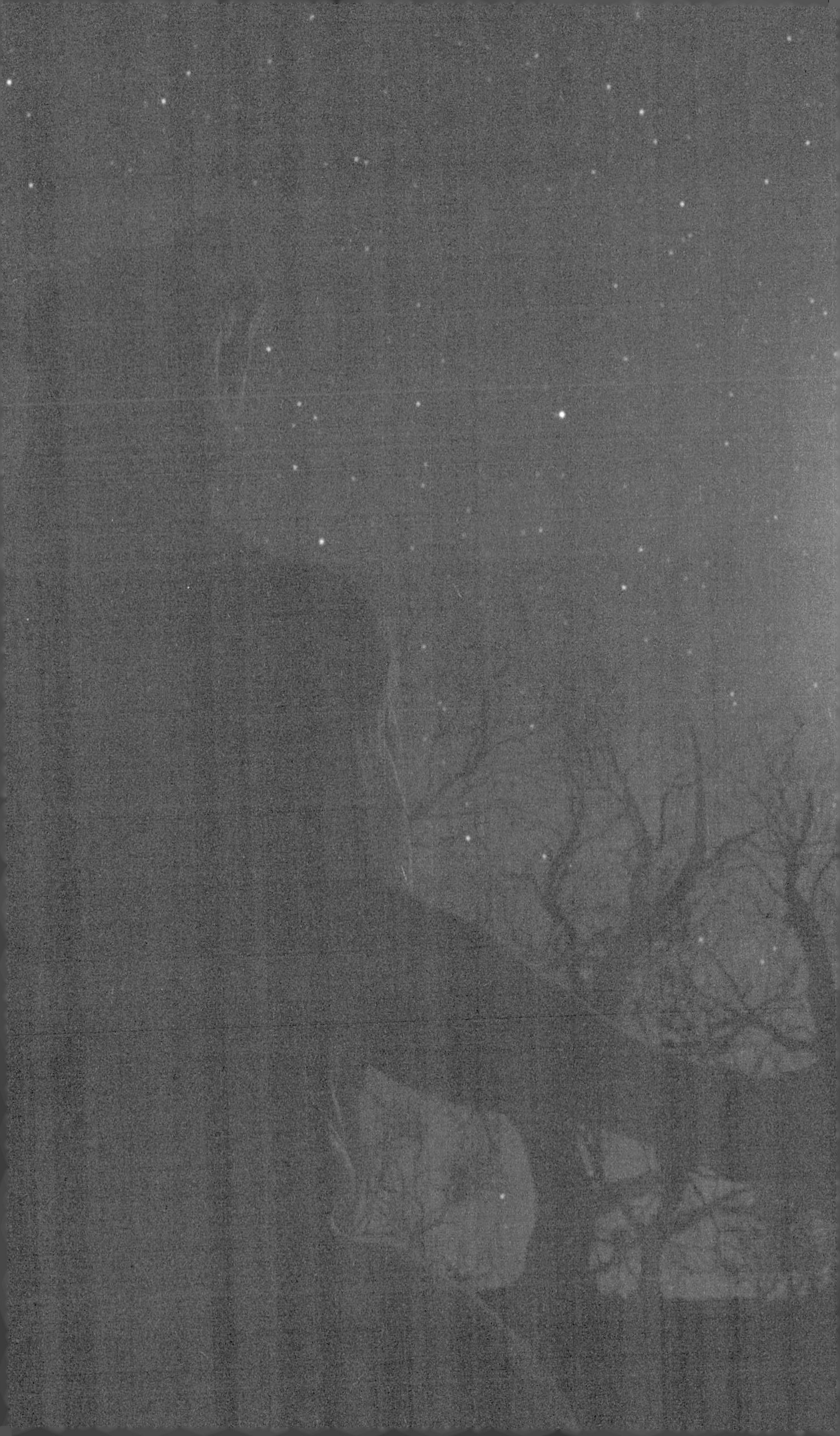

CHAPTER TWELVE

VALLEY OF GHOSTS, NORTHERN WYOMING TERRITORY

The five men stood around the fire and observed the young man they had just untied. Takanawa had cut him off some buffalo jerky, and the boy ate, eyeing his new captors. He kept a close eye on the youngest of the five men while the Brazilian reloaded his pistol.

"Now, boy, do you mind telling us about the companion you travel with? Is he some magical beast or just a man?"

The boy spit out the remains of the jerky and looked at Jackson with seething anger. "Why, so you can kill him?"

"As you see, boy, we are very capable of doing just that." Freemantle indicated toward the body of Alexandros lying fifty feet away.

The young man glanced up at a grinning Porteguee Frank, who closed the cylinder on his Colt, spun the weapon, and holstered it, emphasizing his eagerness and willingness to duplicate the act. The boy's eyes went to each man in this strangest of gatherings. The confusion of the turbaned Sikh, to the top-knotted hair of the Asian, and the weariness of the two men who had a soldier's bearing made the boy wonder what manner of men the Khan had hired to kill his own brother.

Freemantle stuck his booted foot out and harshly nudged the

kid in the arm, nearly knocking him over. "Come on, boy. Start speaking, or we'll just leave you to the cold."

"The man that has hired you—"

"Let's get this straight, young man," Singh interrupted. "I, for one, a man of Her Majesty's armed forces, do not hire out, as you say. I was ordered here, as were a few others. We were told of a bounty and a race to be the first to kill an animal. Now, please answer the colonel's question. Tell us what you know." Singh was losing patience with the slow pace of answers.

"When you killed that pig of a man, you made a mistake and allowed another to escape back to the man that hired you. When this man learns of your treachery, he will take it rather badly. While holding me will bring my father here, I am afraid you will also draw the ire and attention of the real beast."

"You say someone escaped to warn our benefactor?" Singh stepped closer to the boy and knelt. "Who was it?"

"For professionals, you seem to be blind to what you have been chasing through the wilderness. You haven't noticed the strange tracks of the small ones?"

"Yes, we have," Jackson said. "What made those tracks?"

"My father calls them vampyrs. Vampires to you, I guess."

"I do not know this word," said a confused Takanawa.

Singh stood and took a step back. He pursed his lips. "According to legend, they are ancient blood drinkers."

"That's what the Khan would have you believe. But they are simply creatures of his own creation. Stolen children. Dwarves, the unwanted of society. Trained to kill, track, and obey every command of their master. My father told me of them, but even I didn't believe it until I saw them with my own eyes." The boy stood and eased closer to the fire, not fearing a bullet any longer. "And from what the dead servant Alexandros said, the one you let run off was his master's favorite. So, my brave fools, you have either my father to deal with, or you'll have not only a horde of vampyr, but also the beast called Trelzinon Khan."

He rubbed his hands together, realizing he didn't have to fear death from these strangers. By the looks in their eyes, they believed every word he had just told them.

"The absolute truth now, boy." Singh stepped closer and leaned in. "What is it we face?"

The boy swallowed, about to divulge the secret he vowed never to repeat to anyone on earth. He looked around him, at the men waiting for his reply.

"The stories, the myths, and legends of the Old World are not as accurate as tales go. They have been altered through the years to cover up the real truth from ancient times. The two men, they are brothers. My father, Placeous Lupa, the White, being the younger and more human of the two. His older brother, the man that has brought you here, is Trelzinon Khan, the Black."

"You're trying my patience, boy," Colonel Jackson hissed.

"They are what legend calls werewolves. You face the remains of a species created long, long ago through the black magic of Carthage."

The men were silent, absorbing the impossible story as told to them by the boy. In the boy's eyes and demeanor, it was evident, even if a myth, he believed it.

"Old wives' tales," Freemantle said. "Stories to scare children into behaving."

"In a matter of hours, I guess we'll know for sure," the boy said.

"Gentlemen, until we try our escape from this mess, may I suggest we group together?" Jackson said.

Through their silence, they all agreed.

"Should we try and warn the inspector? He could be walking right into the middle of this thing," Singh asked of no one in particular.

"I'm afraid nothing is going to persuade our British friend from the task he has at hand. No, we can only hope that there may be more than just one monster out there," said Colonel Jackson.

"If it's your father who shows up first, young man, explain that we were not responsible for your abduction. At least give us a momentary fighting chance at defending ourselves." Singh gently took Johnathan's arm.

"Maybe you're taking this manure a little too literally," Freemantle suggested. After the war he had just fought and lost, Freemantle found it hard to believe the world could throw this at him.

"Nonetheless, one or the other will be here tonight. Let us pray it's my father."

"Okay, gentlemen," Colonel Jackson said, "let's start to fort up. We just may need a new battle plan."

The five men and their newly freed captive moved with a purpose. But it was Porteguee Frank who said aloud what everyone might have been thinking in their own language.

"Madre de Dios!"

TWENTY MILES SOUTH OF THE VALLEY OF GHOSTS

A lone rider eased into camp. He suspected what might be awaiting him, but he rode forward, nonetheless. The man examined the luxurious tent. He had found what he had been searching for.

Sir Niles Van-Pattenson pulled on the reins, and his mount came to a stop. He watched for any movement within the silent campsite, then tied off his pack mule and slid from his saddle. Van-Pattenson eyed the Springfield rifle but decided it might not be worth the sour welcome he would receive from the one he hoped would be a generous host.

"Hello in the camp," he called out, not too loudly, but not meekly either. "I am sorry to intrude, as I seek a man whose acquaintance may be beneficial to all concerned." He stood silently by his horse, listening for a reply.

None was forthcoming.

"Most beneficial to myself especially." He took a few cautious steps forward.

No smoke rose from the small cast iron chimney, which seemed strangely out of place for the area. Surely, this must have been the right campsite. Van-Pattenson continued until he reached the closed flap of the large tent. He eased back the left side.

"I hope I'm not intruding, but I am a traveler seeking a gentleman who invited me to this marvelous wilderness." He observed the cold interior of the ornate living quarters.

"You have disappointed me, sir. I thought you would have been the one gentleman to have followed instructions."

The deep bass voice sounded from behind him. Van-Pattenson startled but refused to show it. He backed out of the deserted tent and faced the man he had come to meet.

"I received no clear orders, other than the invitation. I was denied the privilege of further instruction in St. Louis by a man claiming to be your assistant."

"Yes, well, he was short on following my explicit orders. I am currently making staffing adjustments."

Van-Pattenson studied the large man. The hair was tousled, and he seemed exhausted. For as cold as it was, the giant wore no coat, only a shirt with red long johns underneath. The man could have been mistaken for what the Americans called a lumberjack.

"You do know that being here and not out there, doing what it is I brought you here to do, makes for a very awkward situation, right, Mr. Van-Pattenson?" The large man made clear his anger by the expression in his eyes.

"I very well could not have achieved what it is you desired, as you well know, since I was followed to this country by a man who has made it his personal quest to see me hang or killed at his earliest convenience. So, as you say, I was also caught in an awkward predicament, right, Mister...?"

"My name is no matter to you." This time, the Khan moved quickly and took the wanted mass murderer by the throat, lifting him off the ground. He angrily tossed him, as if a discarded rag, backward and growled, "My children, tear him apart!"

Van-Pattenson hit the snow-covered ground. He was dealing with a man who was as unhinged as himself. Van-Pattenson was shaking off the sudden blow when fifty shapes burst from the tree line. They ran for him.

And then the small creatures stopped as if they had hit a brick wall. Many fell to their knees, while others stared wide-eyed at something he could not see. A lone white-faced dwarf stumbled out of the pine woods to the north. It crashed hard into the legs of the Khan.

The suddenness of the encounter shocked the large man. He quickly reached down and took the small creature—who resembled those frozen in shock around Van-Pattenson—into his arms and moved for the tent flap. Before entering, the giant turned to those surrounding the killer.

"Keep him down. Leave him alive for now." He vanished into the tent.

Van-Pattenson was starting to go numb in his extremities from being face down in the snow. It had been over an hour since the man had vanished inside the tent with whatever the creature was he carried. Finally, the flap opened, and from the dimness of the interior, a deep voice rang out.

"Join us for some wine, Sir Van-Pattenson."

He slowly sat up. The creatures scattered back into the thick pine trees. Van-Pattenson brushed off the snow and stalked hesitantly toward the tent. At the flap, he waited for a killing blow to strike before realizing his fate had already been decided. His eyes adjusted to the sepia light inside.

The large man sat at a makeshift bar, pouring drinks from a crystal decanter. The creature relaxed in a comfortable-looking chair and, to the Englishman's amazement, was smoking a cigar and drinking noisily from a huge wine glass. Van-Pattenson stood stunned at his sudden change of fortune. His host turned and offered him a glass, which he accepted. He sniffed the imported brandy and hastily downed the warm liquid. The large man smiled and refilled the liquor.

"I have started a fire in the stove. Please, warm yourself and accept my sincere apology for my earlier reaction to your very gracious visit to my camp."

This time, Van-Pattenson sipped the rich cognac but hesitated at taking the offered chair, which was only a foot away from the awful-smelling creature. He inhaled, holding it in, and accepted the seating arrangement. Van-Pattenson watched the foul thing and half raised his glass in toast. The monster just grinned and took a puff of the smelly cigar.

"Please excuse my children outside"—the Khan rubbed the bald head of the creature sitting next to him—"and inside. They can be rather exuberant. My fault. I spoil them so."

"Not at all. No need to apologize for what is clearly a misunderstanding." Van-Pattenson again downed the burning cognac. "May I?" he asked, holding out his empty glass.

His host kindly refilled it and stood before him.

"I am feeling better than I had been an hour ago and have decided to be the gracious host once again. You see, it was a long night, and I was quite put out by your appearance here. But I digress, sir. I was worried about my child here." He again lovingly touched the white-faced creature on its bald head. "And as I anticipated, he brought back what my American friends call 'a mixed bag' of information. As they say, a good news, bad news scenario of sorts on the current status of my contest. I must say, things have gone awry. Thus, I may require your assistance. It seems I have lost my loyal servant, Mr. Alexandros, whom I believe you met east of the Mississippi River in St. Louis. I have lost him to a despicable act—a betrayal, if you will. One engineered by the very man chosen for my beloved contest."

Van-Pattenson recognized an opening, the very one he had hoped to get upon gambling on this meeting. He sipped his drink, and though he wanted to hurriedly agree to anything, he held back his temptation.

"I will be seeking a man of your ability. If you survive what is to come, of course."

"I am listening."

"Your duties will be to do my bidding, as had been the duty of my now-deceased servant, Mr. Alexandros. You will be returning with me to Rumania, whereupon you will resume your duties. Your compensation...Well, let's just say, it is substantial. And the so-called bonuses of your employment will have benefits fitting your...well, let's just say, your nocturnal hobbies and without interference from the outside world."

"Until then, may I assume we have substantial problems in the near future?" Van-Pattenson asked, finishing his drink.

"None that you are not capable of handling. I personally will do what they call 'the hard part.' My familial problems end here. They end now." The large man refilled Van-Pattenson's glass. "Now, shall we make ready to do what we were both born to do?"

"And who is it we will be killing?" he asked, accepting the drink.

"Who is it we will be killing, besides my traitorous contestants, my old friend?" the Khan asked a smiling Raleck.

The small vampyr grinned and hissed. "Brother, brother. Tonight, we kill Placeous! We tear him apart!" Raleck crushed the still-burning treat of cigar in his clawed hand.

"And you will have the honor and privilege of killing the man that has chased you from the comforts of your home, Sir Van-Pattenson."

The Englishman drained his drink, stood, and offered his hand to the Khan, who took it.

"It will be a pleasure to serve you...my master."

The sun lay low atop the Rockies. Running Horse walked away from the cold camp he and Walking Elk had set up above the small rise. They had spent the late afternoon watching the single large tent in the clearing below. The newcomer entered the flap, and the big man, who had at first treated the man with hostility, actually turned his anger into hospitality, confusing the Sioux warrior. They had also observed the many small creatures, counting their number at close to ninety.

Running Horse refused to share his concern with the younger member of his tribe. Instead, he sat cross-legged and silent while the sun started to vanish. The older man's eyes began to close.

Moments earlier, he had swallowed a wooden cup of herb tea supplied to him by Red Cloud at Fort Laramie. The tea had been swallowed cold, and Running Horse had insisted on a chilly camp that evening. The great warrior's eyes started to move underneath the closed lids. The horrid-tasting tea was having its desired effect.

Running Horse was beginning to dream walk.

Walking Elk had heard rumors of strange magic that could send a warrior into a dream state, allowing him to speak to his dead ancestors dwelling in the realm of the departed. The boy stood and gently placed a red blanket around the shoulders of the dreaming man, then eased away, gathering his quiver of arrows and his white, man-made steel hatchet. Walking Elk also took the ancient ball and cap Colt's Dragoon pistol. He backed away into the twilight.

Running Horse found himself in a pure white environment. There was no up or down, no sideways. He could not even feel the ground beneath his feet. It was as if he floated above the purity of whiteness. The dream walk was silent. Not even the sound of his breathing, the pounding of his heart, nor the blood rushing through his extremities was heard. It was as if rabbit fur had been stuffed in all his orifices. Running Horse felt neither cold nor heat. Gone were his warm winter clothing of leather leggings and agency red shirt. He was in a loin cloth and his bone and feather breastplate and bore a single eagle feather in his unbound hair. His only weapon was the quiver of arrows without arrowheads, his bow, and the knife in its tasseled leather sheath on his hip. He stood motionless.

"*This is the way a warrior goes into battle,*" the unseen voice said, seemingly from his own head.

Running Horse looked around the stillness of his surroundings. He was still standing alone.

"*Your enemy will not be killed by the white man's weapons, but by his desire for riches. Look to the shine of silver in the night, when life is threatened as never before.*"

Running Horse recognized who spoke to him. It was his grandfather, the man who had taught him his warrior ways as a child. His father had believed in the new way of warfare, imitating the killing prowess of the white man, but his grandfather taught him as best he could about the degradation of all his people in fighting with the white soldier's dishonor.

"Grandfather, I cannot see you. I have lost my family. Do they follow you to the mother home and walk with you?"

Silence.

"Grandfather?"

"*Your family travels between the winds, grandson. They departed the world of our people without the blessing of the Great Spirit because they were killed by an evil that has walked the earth for century upon century. Until his time on this earth is finished, your family cannot live amongst our ancestors nor commune with the Great Spirit. This deed must be done by their only remaining loved one. It is you, my son.*"

"What weapon can defeat such evil, Grandfather?"

"*This I have seen. You must see it yourself—a riddle, wrapped in leather, wrapped in another riddle. You will look for the shining stars on a white man's saddle. What is a circle can be sharp as a blade."*

"I do not understand, Grandfather. The riddle is finding no hold in my head. Is it because I am not worthy of your wisdom?"

"Your walk in the spirit world is passing, my son. The young one is proving himself worthy in your eyes. This you must stop. His spirit is in danger of walking with those killed by this evil, as with your family. The boy will walk between the winds."

"Grandfather?"

"Wake, my son!" The disembodied voice was as deep as a white man's cannon shot.

The white world around him crumbled like ice from a frozen waterfall. His eyes opened. The sun was now totally absent from the sky. The moon was rising. His grandfather's prophecy was true. Walking Elk was nowhere to be seen.

Then the great howl of a wolf shattered the stillness of the night.

The last day of the contest had begun.

The five men had their horses and mules tied off inside the makeshift circle of packs and shoveled snow. Jackson, Singh, and Freemantle had achieved the best planning they could in forting up the small valley. They had clear fields of fire in all directions and had used the last of their coal oil to spread among the first line of pine, encircling the camp to assist in backlighting any oncoming threat.

The salvation they hoped for was to convince the boy's adoptive father they were no threat to the boy, nor even himself. But would they have the time needed to persuade an obviously crazed father of the truth, that they had been deceived into participating in the contest by lies? In the center of the small ramparts of snow and packs stood the boy, Johnathan. Beside him, in order to make sure no harm came to him, was Porteguee Frank, ready with scoped rifle and his twin Colt revolvers.

The deep howl sounded. First from the south and then another from the near north. Freemantle, Singh, and Jackson chambered rounds into their rifles. Takanawa eased his shiny blade from its wooden scabbard. The partial full moon broke free of the mountaintops, casting the world of night into preternatural twilight.

The world around the contestants became as still as a painting. Evil was close.

CHAPTER THIRTEEN

Running Horse wore the loin cloth, eagle bone breastplate, moccasins, mid-thigh leggings, and the single feather in his hair, like his dream walk had commanded. He watched the large tent from the tree line. There was a steady stream of darker smoke against the night sky, curling up and out from the inside. Many tracks indented the snow, and Running Horse pinpointed the recognizable tell of the impressions laid by his young companion, Walking Elk.

The boy had approached cautiously, pausing to observe the tent and its possible occupants. All around were the smaller footprints of the leather-booted creatures Running Horse now knew served the beast. They were all around.

The outcome of his search would be futile. The scent of coppery blood already wafted through the night air.

Unlike his dream walk vision, he slowly eased an arrow from the quiver at his back. He notched the thin birch tree shaft onto his deer-gut bowstring, then approached the spacious tent of his quarry. His eyes constantly moved without his head turning away from the enclosure. He stepped up to the opening, finally examining the terrain, fearing ambush by the creatures of the forest. Using just the flint arrowhead, Running Horse easily parted the tent's flap.

In the glow of the open stove, a tear in the back of the tent was illuminated. The entire rear was open to the elements. The moon's radiance outside provided bright light, creating a surreal effect.

The body of Walking Elk hung upside down from the center tent pole. His feet had been speared to the wood by a large knife in an evil, upside-down crucifixion. Running Horse had seen something similar on the necklaces of the white priests visiting the villages of his people. The young warrior's throat had been sliced deep and to the bone, and his blood had stained the tarp flooring red. His young arms dangled at his sides in mock surrender.

Running Horse momentarily lost his desire for revenge. He allowed himself to bow his head at the shame he felt for treating the young one with such disdain. And now he had discovered how truly courageous his young follower had been. The drawn arrow and bowstring went lax in his hands.

The young warrior's body had been left as a perverted gift to him by the beast he had been seeking.

After a moment of self-pity over the loss of innocence, Running Horse angrily pulled a chair over and, with his knife, cut the boy's bonds. He eased him down, careful not to drop Walking Elk. Running Horse hurriedly brushed the large buffet table free of silver chafing dishes and empty crystal glasses, where a marvelous buffet of delicacies had been served. The great warrior noticed the bottle of white man's whiskey and slapped off the crystal top of the decanter. He then spread the liquid over the young warrior, splashed it onto the tarps of the tent, and tossed the bottle into the other decanters of fine alcohol, smashing them to allow their contents to flow.

Running Horse walked to the stove and, with his muscled leg, kicked it over. The wooden embers tumbled across the floor. The material instantly roared to life with a heat the Sioux warrior had never felt. He angrily and purposefully stalked toward the ripped rear of the large tent, just as the entirety of the interior whooshed in a ball of noise and flame.

Running Horse would now accept the challenge of the beast and its minions and end this, even unto his own death.

The night had become abnormally silent inside the cover of the humble redoubt. Every man suspected they were being observed, but by what or whom, they could only guess.

"This is worse than waiting for orders to move forward across the cornfield at Gettysburg," Freemantle kneeled and placed two boxes of .44 shells at his knee for rapid reloading.

Captain Singh had gone as far as removing his heavy coat, exposing the bright red uniform blouse of Her Majesty's Bengal Lancers. The same could be said for the samurai, Takanawa. He had taken off his bearskin coat and was dressed in his finest silk robes. A bright red sash crossed his waist, and his bound hair had been freed, then held in place by a headband of black and gold. If he perished that night, he would do so in the tradition of the samurai and die in the way of ancient Bushido—the warrior's death.

As for Porteguee Frank, he only removed his coat, adjusted his tasseled hat, and kissed the crucifix he left to dangle close to his heart. He had pre-loaded six extra cylinders of ball ammunition for the fight he knew was coming. And for the first time in his young life, he realized he was on the right side of things. What a wonderful dime novel this night would make.

"Señor Johnathan, if you survive this night, tell your compadres the story of how Frank Morales left this life," he asked of the boy kneeling at his side.

Johnathan smiled and wondered what had given the Brazilian the notion any of them would walk away from the fight to come. Instead of voicing that concern, he said, "There will be no need for me to tell anyone, Mister Morales. Word will spread of the goings on here in the Valley of Ghosts. Your reputation will surely grow into legend before word of this night reaches the borders of your homeland."

Porteguee Frank didn't respond. He just smiled and adjusted his twin Colts in their silver, concho-covered holsters.

A wisp of cloud passed by the moon now close to its zenith. The nighttime orb seemed to be three times as big as any of the men could remember.

The sound of some instrument pierced the night air. It might have been a clarinet; the men could not be sure. Before they could even contemplate it, the first rock flew into the camp, striking near Major Freemantle.

"Damn, that must be their opening salvo of artillery," he said loudly.

A second and third rock came screaming in from the tree line.

The second stone struck Captain Singh in the leg. It was a glancing blow but accurately thrown. Then the air was filled with rocks. They came from all sides, fast enough that several hit the defenders in the backs, chests, and heads.

"By God, that's enough!" Jackson shouted. He raised his rifle, firing into the tree line at a rapid rate.

Freemantle joined him while ducking incoming fire.

Singh quickly aimed at movement and, with accuracy, shot one of the small creatures, which had tried to creep closer for a more meaningful throw. The vampyr fell, clutching its chest, then remained silent and still.

Porteguee Frank forsook his practiced aim and sacrificed accuracy for speed of fire. With his thumbs working like the arms of a second hand on the finest of watches, his twin Colt revolvers released twelve shots in rapid succession. The pleasurable sound of a yelp told him he had hit something. He reached for his gun belt for another two cylinders, but Johnathan had already retrieved them and was holding out his two reloads. Within ten seconds, Morales was firing into the night once more.

"We need that tree line lit a-fire before those little bastards get their bearings!" Freemantle called out.

Everything was a blur of silk, yellow, and gold in color. Takanawa grabbed the low-wick lantern and jumped free of the small walls of the enclosure. With samurai sword in one hand and flame in the other, he expertly dodged the thrown rocks of their small enemy and shot forward. Soon, fifteen of the vampyrs noticed the danger coming at them and charged the lone man with the long knife.

Takanawa, without breaking stride toward the first of the tall pines, swung the sword with such speed and force, several of the vampyrs didn't even realize they had been sliced in half by the magnificent steel blade of the ancient sword. One of them fell face-first into the snow, but his two legs continued to run for six feet before falling over. Even then, they twitched with imaginary life.

Ten more charged the Japanese warrior and were quickly shot down by the firing of Singh, Freemantle, and Morales. All ten slid to their last breaths in the snow. Takanawa sliced the heads off five more while pausing momentarily to fight them off. Then five additional creatures went down in pieces against the samurai sword Takanawa flashed in the bright moonlight.

Finally, an opening formed, and he ran. Takanawa raised his left arm to the sky to throw the burning lantern into the first of the trees. He never made it. Five vampyrs swarmed him from above. They jumped screaming, with pure murderous excitement, from their hiding places in the pines. The vampyrs covered the samurai and started stabbing at him with small blades.

The men paused in their defense.

Takanawa, highlighted by the moon, swung his sword wildly, even managing to dislodge three of the small creatures. His efforts became slower as the vampyr gained the upper hand through sheer numbers and knife thrusts. Takanawa went down to his knees and slowly fell forward. More bullets struck his assailants. Thirteen additional vampyr went down before Takanawa's body was dragged off. Even five of those creatures succumbed to well-aimed bullets from Freemantle, Jackson, Morales, and Singh.

Captain Singh lowered his empty Webley pistol and closed his eyes. He said a soft prayer to the Sikh god, Waheguru, the one true god of East Indian mysticism. Then he surprised his companions by following Takanawa out of the small enclosure.

"Damn it, cover the man!" Jackson shouted.

Even Johnathan took one of the spare rifles and started to fire at any movement, other than the red-uniformed Sikh.

At least twelve more of the vampyrs went down. Singh didn't have much time. He dove the last five feet of space and almost broke the glass of the lantern. When he secured it, he stood, cocked his arm, and threw the glass-enclosed flame. It hit the first pine with a precise strike, exploding against the cold wood with a loud pop.

Just when he lofted the flame, more vampyr grabbed for the larger man. One, maybe two were shot off the struggling Sikh, but there were too many. Twenty of them dragged Singh away, hitting him ruthlessly while they did so.

Captain Singh tried desperately to grab anything, hoping to free himself from the terror taking him to the most unholy of deaths. But all his hands came away with were snow and pine needles. The blows to his head and torso were beginning to exert their toll on his consciousness. Luckily, his thick red uniform jacket blunted most of the knives' blades.

Then the dragging and hitting stopped. Singh could barely detect the warmth of the blaze he had only moments before started. The fire had spread to first one tree and then the next, and then the next. His eyes started to close, and he knew he had achieved what he wanted in the last act of his life. His honor was complete.

His mind started to drift. His knee-high boots lifted free of the ground, and he momentarily swung like a pendulum. His body rose higher, then stopped. He had been hung upside down from one of the interior trees.

"That is quite high enough," came a voice from a man Singh couldn't see. "Leave me to my work. Join the others and assist your master. I have other matters to attend to."

The vampyrs retreated, following the unseen man's orders. The voice was not familiar to Singh, other than the fact the accent was that of an Englishman. That brought two persons to mind: either Inspector Tensilwith or the man he had pursued, the famed Butcher of Whitehall. Knowing the man from Scotland Yard would never affiliate himself with the small creatures, Singh suspected his last moments of life would be filled with agony at the hands of the one who had terrorized Londoners for the past three years.

"Captain Singh. I must apologize for not meeting you and your companions in St. Louis. I so wanted to. But alas, sir, I was warned not to linger after my brief but profitable tour of that very fine city."

Singh's body spun slowly around. Although upside down, he could now see the man clearly. His beard was well-trimmed, and of all things, he wore clothes befitting a lush ball in the standards of London society. Singh sighed. His death was coming in a surreal nightmare of unbelievable proportions.

"Come, Captain. Do not expire before we complete our task for this evening. You may be the only one I confront tonight, after my new associate is finished with the others."

Singh's red tunic was torn free of its gold- and silver-plated buttons. His pure white turban was slowly unwound, freeing his long, black hair. A knife blade gently slid up his chest to his belt, followed by a few taps of the sharp instrument.

The man started to hum a tune Singh did not know, and the knife pierced his shoulder slowly. The blade sank deep into the muscle, the pain building and his nerves finally responding to the assault. The warm blood ran down his chest, across his face, and finally into his swaying hair.

"You know, Englishmen can be so cruel in their understanding of other races. Some would be surprised that you have red blood, the same as them. Most times, I despise my own species, Captain Singh. But we men of action know the truth of all things. Do we not, sir?"

"I...would not...be a...blasphemer...by...saying you can...go straight...to...hell!" Singh said as strongly as he could.

Van-Pattenson laughed as though it was the funniest thing he had ever heard. "Well, if you believe in that sort of nonsense, I would most assuredly be going there. But not as soon as many would like, Captain."

This time, the blade sank deep into his thigh. The pain was excruciatingly bright. Singh hissed, refusing to give this butcher the thing he wanted: his screams.

"Hell? I would undoubtedly be ruling there soon after my arrival and my greeting with old Lucifer, a man that I have admired for his wonderful tales of deceit and death." Van-Pattenson laughed.

"Then allow me to make the introductions just a little sooner than you anticipated!"

A swift swooshing sound ended in a clang like a large cowbell. Van-Pattenson yelped when his body hit the ground. A single shot rang out. A shovel came into view, and the spade was shoved deep into the snow below Singh.

His weight fell free of the ropes holding him. Before Singh hit the earth, hands and arms arrested his fall. He opened his eyes to the familiar face of former Chief Inspector Robert Tensilwith.

"Sorry I was late, old boy. Got caught up by those nasty little bald-headed buggers. Had a hell of a time weeding them out of my way." He half lifted Singh and then allowed him to catch his breath. "As I was—"

Tensilwith grunted and quickly fired four more shots from his Webley pistol.

Van-Pattenson stood, holding his stomach where first one, then four more bullets fired by Tensilwith had buried deeply into his body. The man grinned, with blood coursing down his lips.

"You think you have...ended...my reign...?" he gasped.

Tensilwith took a step forward and placed his last bullet directly in the center of the Butcher of Whitehall's forehead. The man simply fell backward, the back of his head blown out.

"Yes, I am pretty sure your reign has come to an end." Tensilwith turned. "Shall we try and make our way to the others, Captain? It sounds as if they're having the devil's all, with all of the shooting going on." He reached down and hissed but then managed to get Captain Singh on his feet.

THE CONTEST

It was after only forty feet they came across the mutilated corpse of Takanawa. Clutched in his dead fingers was the ancient samurai sword given to him by the head of his prefecture back home. A few feet away was one of the dead vampyrs.

"Retrieve the sword. I will make sure to get it back to his home in Japan. We owe him at least that much," Singh said, one arm around the inspector's shoulder.

With the sword in Tensilwith's possession, both exhausted men knew it would be a battle fighting their way back to the clearing.

Empty cartridge cases covered the snow at their feet. Porteguee Frank had used all his extra cylinders and had recruited young Johnathan to reload them. Freemantle and Jackson had emptied four cartridge cases of .44-40 ammunition and were still letting loose volley after volley in rapid-fire shot and then ejection. In front, rear, and both sides of the clearing, dead and dying vampyrs bled in the bright moonlight. Their warm blood created a ground fog where it met snow.

The main assault had commenced right after Takanawa had gone down. When Captain Singh successfully ignited the tree line, the small creatures had charged with screaming menace. And still there was no sign of the beast that had sent them on their suicidal mission to diminish the men's forces.

"To the front!" Jackson yelled loudly, over the cacophony of rifle and pistol fire.

Just breaking from the trees, two men staggered, fell, recovered, and then stumbled forward—Captain Singh, obviously seriously wounded, and another man supporting him. Four vampyrs took notice and redirected themselves from their charge at the entrenched men to the wounded one and his escort. Singh stumbled once more. His fall created an opening for the man trying to help him to pull his pistol and quickly dispatch three of the four dwarves.

"Porteguee, take that little bastard down!" Freemantle screamed, hurriedly reloading his empty Henry.

Porteguee Frank moved to the front of the enclosure and let loose a hail of gunfire, shaking the world around them. At least eight shots of ball ammunition shrieked forward and took the head off the charging vampyr. Morales immediately turned to get more cylinders for his empty pistols.

The two men were once more fighting their way to safety. Both Jackson and Freemantle, now reloaded, started to give them withering cover fire. When they made it to the makeshift wall of the small fortress, Morales quickly stopped firing and reached over the wall of snow and supplies. He pulled first Singh and then, to all three men's surprise, former Chief Inspector Tensilwith over the crumbling wall of protection.

"Thank you, gentlemen. It was getting rather sticky for a moment there," Tensilwith said, out of breath.

"Welcome back." Jackson fired two rapid shots, bringing two more of the creatures down. "I assume Scotland Yard got their man?"

"You assume correctly, Colonel. However, I don't believe I'll be staying long in your gentlemen's outstanding company."

The chief inspector, seemingly in slow motion, fell forward until he crashed headfirst onto the legs of the man he had just saved, a large knife in his back. Singh, very much in pain from his torturous wounds, eased the man over and placed a hand on his head, closing Tensilwith's eyes. He pursed his lips and mumbled a silent prayer for the man who had pulled him from the gates of Hell.

"Damn it all!" Jackson fired three more shots.

"Yes, he got his man, but Van-Pattenson had one killing left in him," Singh said. "He assisted me all the way back while he himself was dying." Among the gunfire and fear of the moonlit night, Singh brushed a lock of the inspector's hair from his face. "Go now, friend. Be with your wife. She awaits."

Porteguee Frank slammed home a freshly reloaded cylinder into his steaming Colt. He looked at the two men on the ground—one dead, the other most assuredly on his way to join him. That was when Morales realized what death was really about, the cold hardness that had been his life. He experienced shame for the first time.

Morales would never deserve to have his exploits put to ink and paper. No one wanted to read about a coward whose only claim to fame was the murder of starving and poor people. In anger, Morales lifted the freshly loaded Colt and emptied it at the dwindling targets now stumbling to their deaths. Three of the six shots missed, his eyes blurry with tears.

The last shot was fired at a still moving but downed vampyr. The night became still. The gun smoke lingered in the breezeless night, and a surreal sense of impending danger settled over the enclosed camp.

Jackson broke the spell of false silence and moved to the side of the chief inspector. Tensilwith was long past assistance, a serene look of peace on his face. The man had done what he had traveled to the New World to do. Jackson hoped someday he would be able to find that sense of peace after years of blood and death.

"He was a good man, Captain Singh," Jackson said, finally looking up.

Captain Singh sat with his eyes open, but there was no life in him. The long black hair was matted with blood, and his head had slipped to the side. His hand was still on the gentle features of Chief Inspector Tensilwith. Jackson reached over and closed the Sikh's eyes.

"Ah, damn it to hell." Colonel Jackson slowly stood; his rifle crooked in his arm. He looked at Freemantle, who reloaded his rifle, to Morales who was doing the same, not looking up for anything. Then Jackson noticed the accusing eyes of the orphan boy, Johnathan. His face was expressionless. Each had died because they all had refused to disobey an order from inferior men, which made them just as bad as the beast they hunted. Jackson turned away.

Jackson walked to the ramparts of their small castle and surveyed the dead vampyr army. Some lay in heaps; some lay alone. No matter what they were, they had been used too. Used by a monster with no real love for anything, other than the destruction of all that could be good in the world. Jackson glanced at the remainder of the contestants. They were nearly cut from the same mold as the beast, who would kill them all that night.

He started to turn away from the killing fields surrounding them, when he froze.

The roar, a scream of pure evil, came from somewhere in the trees.

Each man cringed. Giant tree after giant tree came crashing to the ground. The beast was there and had seen the destruction of his dwarf army. Another roar ripped the sky, like unseen lightning. Then another. But it was the howl of sadness following that gave all three men and the boy cold chills.

The bringer of death was now coming for them, for their betrayal.

CHAPTER FOURTEEN

Running Horse's mostly naked body was not cold. He knelt to one knee and traced a finger in and around the large prints in the snow. The warrior knew them well. He had seen them all his life—the tracks of Brother Wolf. But these tracks were at least five times the size of any he had ever seen.

By the depth of them, this animal weighed more than six hundred pounds, the weight of a young bull Tatanka. But this beast was more than a match for even the mightiest buffalo. These tracks were made by the evil spirit that had killed his entire family. He had also disgraced the young warrior who was learning to become a man.

Running Horse stood. His dark eyes roamed over the remains of the small bodies he now understood were at this great beast's calling. Their wounds, a trace of the white men he thought might be in league with his quarry...It didn't matter. If the white man hindered him in any way, he would also die.

It had been at least fifteen minutes since the distant shooting had stopped. Either the white intruders to his lands had perished, or there was a lull in the battle.

That was when he heard the roar and howls. Running Horse knew exactly where the rage cracking the sky came from. He didn't hesitate. His eyes followed the tracks, confirming his direction.

The fires in the trees had started to diminish. The bright oranges and reds were fading when two of the smoldering pines came crashing down.

"I guess the curtain is going up on this warped little Passion Play of ours," Freemantle said.

"Would seem so, my Confederate comrade." Jackson harshly chambered a fresh round into his large Henry rifle. "Boy..." Jackson took aim at where the two pines had crashed into the snow, covering several of the dead vampyrs. "It seems your Pa isn't coming to your rescue, so you have permission to skedaddle."

Johnathan stood with a spare Henry in hand. Porteguee Frank shook his head.

"Largo de aqui, kid," he said in Spanish.

But the boy had no intention of "getting out of there." Johnathan also chambered a bullet.

An expanse of blackness appeared before they could fully realize what they were seeing. Their eyes traveled up the beast before them. The chest was as broad as a wagon's seat, the legs thicker than most of the trees surrounding them. The ears were tall and pointed, and the muzzle was as black as coal. Its chest heaved in and out like a great bellows. The bright yellow eyes were focused on them, and it was as if heat emanated from the ancient beast's hatred, not just of them, but of all living things that might have been created through the natural order of God's selection process.

"Madre de Dios." Morales crossed himself with pistol in hand.

"This may not turn out for the best here, gentlemen," Jackson said.

The giant werewolf stared with pure hate and evil.

"Okay, I guess we all owe you an apology, son," Freemantle admitted. "It seems we judged you a little too soon about fairy tales and such."

"I guess I always had a grain of doubt about my father's stories, so don't feel too bad, Major."

The monster's eyes never wavered from the spot where the men stood their ground. It took its first step forward, then a second and a third.

"Are you waiting for another invitation, señors?" Porteguee Frank yelled. His twin Navy Colts started blasting away at the not-so-distant target.

Eight out of the twelve bullets riddled the chest and stomach of the giant beast, but it never lost stride. It shook its massive black head and came on even faster. Six more large-caliber rounds from three Henry rifles found their mark, one even slamming into the head of the werewolf. It sent the muzzle into the air, only to straighten with more fiery determination in its eyes. It roared again in anger at the defiance of the men he had hired to do a job they had so richly failed at.

Porteguee Frank reloaded, thought a moment, then broke ranks. He shoved his pistols into his holsters and made a run for where the horses had been hobbled at the center of their camp. Morales quickly cut the hobble ropes and jumped onto his silver-studded saddle. He harshly turned the animal and sprinted for the front of the walled fort. The black stallion easily jumped it, to the amazement of Freemantle, Jackson, and Johnathan. Morales rode hard at the werewolf, knowing he could be more precise with his bullets at a closer range.

"What in the hell is he doing?" Jackson shouted.

The beast stood its ground. Morales charged like J.E.B.

Stuart, the brilliant Confederate cavalry commander during the recent war between the states.

"Boy's got a death wish, for sure," Freemantle answered, even though he was in awe of the way the kid had come around since life had been explained to him by Captain Singh.

Porteguee Frank dropped his black stallion's reins, took both pistols, and started firing at thirty yards from the great beast. Each of his bullets struck home: three in the animal's heart, three to its massive forehead, and three more near its thick neck. Frank screamed in triumph when the beast finally stumbled a few steps back.

It wasn't that the werewolf was hurt. The beast had simply experienced the punch of the large ball rounds striking it. It straightened with an angry roar and shake of its head. When Frank's speeding horse started to ride by the dazed werewolf, it roared again. Its thick arms and claws swung outward, catching Frank and sending him flying from the saddle.

The two silver-plated pistols flew into the air and vanished when the Brazilian hit the ground. The giant werewolf was immediately upon him. The horse never slowed. It sped into the forest, away from the noise and the smell of blood.

The three survivors watched as the young assassin was torn to shreds before their eyes. They knew what was at stake. The three kept up a relentless fire against the creature spawned by black magic over twenty-four hundred years before. The bullets still had no effect.

All that was left from the hopeful hero gunfighter from Brazil was a patch of bright red blood, which would stain and freeze over until April.

Running Horse was sprinting through the pines toward the sound of battle. His breath came in short bursts, and he tried to keep his breathing under control.

Something crashed its way through the underbrush and branches.

Running Horse slid to a stop, drew his bone-handled knife, and waited. His eyes widened when a pure black animal crashed into his view—a horse. He hurriedly threw his hands in the air, trying to halt the animal's flight from battle. The stallion finally slowed and stopped, grateful to see something natural after what it must have witnessed.

The Sioux warrior eased close and rubbed the long nose of the black stallion, whispering softly spoken words to it. He was checking the animal for injuries when he noticed the saddle. His body started feeling strange. The silver conchos lining the leather brought a vision that caught Running Horse off guard. He closed his eyes, not even hearing the distant shots of the white men while they fought the real evil in the world. Running Horse was remembering his dream walk. He concentrated on the familiar voice of his grandfather.

"You will look for the shining stars on a white man's saddle."

The words seemed to echo in his head. He opened his eyes and studied the saddle, failing to find any stars. The only adornments on the blackened leather were the silver conchos lining both saddle and stirrups. Running Horse slowly started to understand the strange words of his grandfather.

Are these the weapons the old one spoke of? But how?

Running Horse remembered the rest of the riddle. *"What is now a circle can be sharp as a blade."* The warrior pulled hard on one of the conchos, freeing it from the thick thread holding it.

Then plucked another, then another, and then finally a fourth. He hoped this would be enough. Time was short for him to act.

He tied the horse to a frozen bush and found a large, snow-covered rock. Running Horse hurriedly removed four arrows from the leather quiver and lay them beside him. He placed the first concho on it, took his knife, and reversed it where the handle would do his work. Running Horse set the concho on edge and slammed the knife handle down hard, partially bending it. He repeated the action.

This time, the concho completely folded over in half. He used the knife handle to slam the concho flat until he had a half-moon shape. Running Horse just hoped the edge was sharp enough for the concho to do whatever work his grandfather had seen. He took an arrow and hurriedly unwound the deer gut holding the arrowhead in place.

Running Horse tied the half-moon-shaped concho to the shaft. He retied the tip and prayed it would hold. The warrior repeated the process with the other three arrows and conchos. His life and that of many other of his people depended on a riddle brought forth by a dream walk. He jumped on the black stallion and sped toward his destiny, following the first of the great beast's roar.

The werewolf had finished its work on Porteguee Frank. Now with blood, flesh, and gore dripping from its black muzzle and six-inch claws, the werewolf turned to the final three killings of the night. It started to trot, then broke into a full sprint of a charge. It came on, even as bullet after bullet struck it. It flew through the air, coming down on Major Freemantle and driving him onto the frozen ground and empty shell casings, freeing all the wind in his lungs.

Jackson and Johnathan both fired everything they had left into the back and head of the animal. They could feel the impact of their bullets, even through their boots. The crack of bone and the thud of rounds hitting the thick, black fur of the beast rang through the air, but the werewolf was wholly concentrating on Freemantle, not noticing its own wounds. It straightened, and its bright yellow eyes narrowed when it saw the boy.

Johnathan pulled the trigger of the Henry rifle.

Click.

The firing pin hit on nothing but emptiness. The beast seemed to smile, showing its four-inch incisors, making a cruel joke of the last minute of the boy's life. It stepped forward. Johnathan let the Henry rifle slip from his frozen grasp. He closed his eyes, preparing for the final assault.

The attack never came.

Jackson was just raising his now-empty rifle into the air, planning to hit the werewolf with the butt end, when a white blur came flying through the space. The white and black rage of fur rolled and crashed through the thin walls of the makeshift fort. They growled, teeth slashing. The black finally kicked its way to a standing position, then turned and faced its attacker.

Placeous Lupa, his brother, stood before him, his snow-white fur bristling with anger. The two great animals roared and hissed, squaring off for the first time in their long history. Trelzinon Khan was the first to raise its muzzle to the moon-filled sky and howl. That was quickly followed by Placeous, who did the same.

Johnathan and Colonel Jackson would have covered their ears, but they were frozen in awe and wonderment at the confrontation of two legendary creatures.

Trelzinon Khan charged his brother. The larger animal struck, sending both backward to the ground. Placeous, shocked at the speed of the attack, recovered quickly. He sank his large teeth into the space between the Black's neck and shoulder. Trelzinon raised its head and screamed out in pain.

Other than shock, the bite didn't really seem to affect the Black. It struck out with the claws of both hands. They slammed into Placeous the White's torso again and again. With every blow, the White was losing his ability to fight back. Trelzinon sank the claws of its right hand into its brother, lifting him free of the ground and throwing him. He landed twenty yards away, hitting the frozen earth with a thud that shook the world around them.

Trelzinon was on him again. The beast was in a rage, consumed by over two thousand years of fear and loathing of a far weaker brother than it ever thought. He had lived in fear for nothing. Trelzinon would end this tonight.

"Father!" Johnathan screamed, trying to run to him.

Jackson caught the boy and held him in place.

Placeous, awaiting his brother's final assault, raised a clawed hand in order to stay the boy's love for him. He held it until Trelzinon attacked. The older brother ripped easily into the last of the powers that could defeat him—his own brother, the last of his kind outside of himself.

Jackson decided it was time to try and run. Just standing there, waiting to be slaughtered, was not his way of thinking.

"Let's go. This fight's over, son."

They both ran. Johnathan fought back tears for the man who had been the only one in his entire life to show him affection. He was now being torn apart by the purest of evil.

The werewolf finally ceased its destruction of its brother. It stood, and the mighty howl of triumph that had been waiting to escape its lungs for thousands of years filled the nighttime sky. It was now feeling young again. Free of worry. No one or thing could ever kill it.

With the howl and the crunch of snow, Jackson knew the werewolf had begun pursuit. When the beast was near, he pushed the boy and himself to the ground. The great black animal flew over them. It crashed and then rolled to its clawed feet.

It would take its time and have fun. The beast started slowly walking toward the last two of its real enemies.

Too late did Trelzinon hear the war whoop of the warrior known as Running Horse. The warrior who had been tempted into joining the contest, unknown by the beast itself. He rode straight up in the white man's saddle, his hair flying backward.

Jackson thought the warrior had gone insane.

Running Horse shouted at the beast. The first silver-tipped arrow flew from the bow. It struck Trelzinon in the upper chest, then quickly a second in the left hip.

Trelzinon took a step forward, but immediately, something slowly started to course through his new wounds, spreading throughout his body. He tried to take a step again, and this time, he nearly stumbled. The Khan roared, but it didn't seem or feel as powerful as before. He tried to stand straight.

The Indian warrior he had severely injured not two months earlier...The warrior he had heard so much about in his time on the Plains slid the black stallion to a stop and was off before the werewolf could flinch.

Trelzinon howled when Running Horse notched his third arrow and let it loose. It struck the black-hearted beast in the center of its chest. Before the yelp of pain had cleared its muzzle fully, the fourth and final concho-tipped arrow struck it in the area covering its heart. The beast made the sound of a severely hurt dog. It tried to roar out its pain but went down to one knee, barely able to hold its own body weight.

Still, the poison was spreading faster and faster from the pure silver conchos of Porteguee Frank's richly adorned saddle. Blood poisoning had never been a fear in the deepest thoughts of the species. They had never realized necromancers in the time of Carthage would always have an instrument of death against the evil they might create. In this case, purest silver.

Running Horse stood before his enemy, his arsenal of silver-tipped arrows depleted. He drew one from the quiver traditionally tipped with volcanic glass. Running Horse made ready to place the arrow as deep into the animal as he could.

Trelzinon whined from deep inside his chest. The great black beast simply fell over into the snow, its blood pouring freely from the quickly festering wounds. The ancient evil one took its final breath.

Running Horse stepped forward. With his knife, he easily sliced the beast's right ear away. He held it to the sky and yelled to his family, who would not walk in between the winds. When done, he put the ear into the top of his leather leggings and angrily turned to Jackson and the boy. He once more drew his bow, aiming it at the two white men.

A curious look came to the warrior's features. He lowered the aim of his arrow only a few inches.

"I know your face," he said in very broken English, looking at Colonel Jackson.

"Yes, we have met, twice. Once before, and then once during the great council of Laramie."

Running Horse fought his memory. He thought he remembered a very much younger soldier.

"I was a young lieutenant back then. You were a boy just learning where he belonged." Jackson looked down at the dead werewolf. "I guess you found out where you fit in."

Running Horse lowered the bow and arrow. His eyes never left the man and boy. The young white man was saddened in some way his wet eyes attested to. Running Horse remembered his young companion, Walking Elk. He took a breath, turned, and started to walk back to the black stallion, who would be his companion all the way through to the Battle of Little Bighorn. Running Horse stopped and faced Jackson.

"Go. Do not come back here, soldier." Running Horse looked around, and his eyes settled on the waning partial moon. Then he glanced at the bodies of the dead vampyr. "This place is filled with the memory of the dead. You will find it if you return." He quickly mounted the stallion and eased it toward the south.

After burying the dead, the boy stood in front of the larger of the graves. The colonel's eyes roamed over the makeshift graveyard, and he shook his head in regret. Lying beside and guarding the great white werewolf were the remains of Captain Singh. Beside him was the body of Chief Inspector Tensilwith. On the other side of Placeous was the smaller grave of Porteguee Frank Morales, the boy who, in the end, had redeemed his soul. And finally, the man that was the furthest from home, Oishi Takanawa.

The great werewolf who had saved their lives would have the very best of guardians at his side, wherever they might end up. Jackson brandished the samurai sword in salute to the brave warrior from the distant land of Japan.

The two men gathered what was left of their supplies, preparing to move south. They slid into their saddles, then readied the two pack mules.

"Here, boy." Jackson tossed a small leather bag toward Johnathan, who deftly caught it. "Took that off the body of our Mister Alexandros. I calculate about five hundred dollars in gold. Should be enough to give you a start anywhere you choose."

"Thank you," the boy said sadly.

Jackson noticed the emotion there but said nothing more. He turned his mount, and the two men headed south.

Three miles into their journey, Jackson allowed the boy to catch up to him.

"Know much about cows? Ranching? That sort of thing?"

"Not much," Johnathan answered.

"Well, you can learn, can't you?" Jackson shot back.

"Reckon I can, yes, sir," the boy answered. "What would we face down in cattle country, Colonel?"

Jackson smiled and tilted his hat back. "Oh, nothin' more than wild Indians, tornadoes, disease. Not much."

"But no werewolves, right?"

"Well, it's Texas, boy. You never know!"

For the first time in what seemed like years, the boy smiled, and Jackson laughed.

THE END

ABOUT THE AUTHOR

DAVID L. GOLEMON was born and raised in Ontario, California, and is a veteran of the U.S. Army. He has called Texas and Colorado home and has raised three great children. David now makes his home on Long Island, New York.